Paths of Power

Initialization
Family Perils

An Initialization Side Story

By Sean Barber

ISBN: 979-8-9858226-6-3

Cover art by: A-P Graphics

Printed in the United States of America

Table of Contents

"Don't forget, Drake is out of school this week; his mom is letting us have him until you go back on the road. He's excited to see you," Rose said to her husband over the phone.

"I am too. This should be a good home time," John said with a smile in his tone.

"Also, if you remember, my parents are coming down from Denver Friday for the barbeque. How long until you get in?" Rose asked.

"Yeah, I know. I'll be home in about a day and a half," John replied.

"Where you at now?" she asked.

"Just passed that sublet place in southern Idaho a bit ago, not too much further to Utah," John answered.

"You're making good time; well, I've got to get back to making salads for the beardies. Krom and Alma are giving me the stink eye," she said with a chuckle. "Love you."

"Love you too, babe, talk to you later."

"Bye."

"Bye."

Rose put her phone down and collected the dishes from the bearded dragon tanks. *I need to get more crickets for the Leo's tomorrow too.* Rose thought, adding one more item to her mental to-do list.

As she walked into the kitchen to prepare the salads, the world seemed to slow down. It was like a moment that got stretched into infinity. As the world around her came to a complete halt, a pale blue box appeared before her eyes.

```
Essence Threshold reached
Beginning System Initialization...
.....
.....
.....
Analyzing...
.....
.....
.....
```

What is going on? Why can't I move? What the hell is happening? Essence threshold? System initialization?

```
Essence Quality: Low
Essence Nature: Chaotic
Sapient Population Levels: Critical
Technology Compatibility: Low
Progression Compatibility: Varied
```

Oh no, John told me about books like this. I even listened to a couple with him when we were team driving. Oh god, no, this can't be happening. I'm just dreaming, right... Right? This is just one of my night terrors, and I will eventually wake up. Everything will be fine.

```
Processing...
Processing...
Accessing cultural history...
Processing...
Processing...
Accessing Global Knowledge Database...
Processing...
Processing...
```

It's not ending. I still can't move. Rose felt like she should be hyperventilating. Her heart should be beating out of her chest, but she wasn't breathing. She couldn't feel her heart beating. Everything but her mind was frozen in place.

Divine entities selected
Arcane system selected
Personal Cultivation selected
Flora mutation initialized
Fauna mutation initialized
Monster spawn initialized
System Initialization Stage 1 Initialized

Congratulations!

Congratulations Sapients, after nearly 3.7 billion years, earth has finally reached the Essence threshold and Can now begin the System Initialization.

Due to the lower-than-expected Essence Density generated by the Sapients on this planet, your population had to reach a critical mass before triggering the Initialization. With a population density so high, a self-extinction event was barely averted. Do not worry, sapient. The System Initialization event will reduce your population sufficiently to avoid the extinction of your species.

After careful analysis, it has been determined that your species, with widely differing cultures, beliefs, and individual proclivities, will have a choice in the Path of Power available to you. Three Paths of Power have been selected; these paths have the highest chance for optimal growth for the most significant number of your populations.

CHOOSE YOUR PATH

Path of Mana

Path of Ki

Path of Faith

What do I do? If this is a dream, do I just wait until I wake up? Yes, I'll try that. I'll just wait until I wake up. I won't choose anything.

Rose stood there, holding the empty food bowls she used for feeding the bearded dragons their salads for what felt like an eternity. Nothing changed. She still couldn't breathe, but she didn't feel starved of oxygen, either. Time just seemed frozen, like no matter how long she stood there, staring at the last blue screen telling her to make a choice, that no time would actually pass.

Ok, I can't just keep standing here reading and re-reading this screen. Nothing is changing; nothing else is happening. I need to think this through. I need to think like John, analyze the information available to me. He went on and on about all those LITrpg books and his cultivation stories. He even roped me into playing D&D with him, his son Drake, and Drake's half-sister Kassie.

Mana is used by mages. I'm not sure what Ki is precisely, but it sounds like Tai Chi or something, and I'm not built for fighting and Faith...

I was done with the church after I turned eighteen. Even if there is some kind of system apocalypse story thing going on... not even the end of the world will not drive me back to that. I'm no fighter. I'm just an overweight woman who likes to take care of and help developmentally disabled people. That's why I started work at the Day program.

If this is real, what will happen to those poor people? How are they going to understand or handle this?

I'm getting distracted. I have to make a choice, or nothing will happen. Fucking ADHD. If Faith and Ki are out, there is only one actual option. Rose chose the Path of Mana.

> You have chosen the Path of Mana

> **Path of Mana**
>
> The raw power to shape the universe is at your fingertips. By shaping mana to your will, you can raise mighty empires or sunder entire civilizations. Your body will be capable of converting ambient essence straight into mana automatically. Choose your base class and slay your enemies. Increase your levels and spend your attribute points.
>
> Attributes must be spent within 24 hours of leveling; if the Attribute points have not been spent in the allotted time, then they will be automatically assigned to the lowest attributes.

Maintaining the power of enhanced attributes within a human body requires a minimum balance, otherwise you may irreparably damage yourself. With this in mind, no one attribute can be more than twice the level of your lowest attribute.

Masters of mana can walk their own path; the classes you choose will evolve with you at certain level thresholds, maximizing your future potential. Threshold levels are 10, 25, 50, 75 and 100. At each threshold, the System will analyze your magic abilities, skill levels and choices made to generate custom advanced classes tailored to you. Choose which new class fits you best, or wait until your next threshold.

Warning: if you pass up your threshold selection, you will forfeit the new or increased bonuses the advanced classes bring.

Base Class Options: **Artisan, Mage, Rogue, Warrior.**

Choose your Class

Artisan

Mage

Rogue

Warrior

Unlike the choice of Paths, each class listed under Base Classes was bolded and seemed 'clickable'. Rose clicked on the Artisan class to see what would happen.

Artisan: not everyone is suited for combat. Artisans are the people specializing in the crafting of items and construction of buildings. Artisans will gain a small amount of experience when crafting items with higher quality items providing greater experience. Artisans receive 1 school of magic, class ability **Arcane Enhancement** and gain extra Mana and Mana regeneration per attribute point. +2 Intelligence, +2 Wisdom, +1 Dexterity

The Artisan class doesn't seem too bad. I am decent at making crystal necklaces with silver wire, crocheting, and a sewing machine. But if this is an apocalypse scenario, will crocheting help us survive? What is Arcane Enhancement? It looks clickable too.

Arcane enhancement: channel your mana while crafting an object. The base materials become more pliable, increasing the chance of higher item quality. Upon completion of a crafting project, the mana invested in the item transforms to enhancement points which can be spent to improve the item characteristics.

That seems like cool class ability. Of course, it would be nice to just sit back and craft things, but I don't think playing with yarn will help keep us alive without John here.

Mage: Mages focus on the art of spell casting. They have the deepest mana pools, and the most potent spells available. Mages receive 2 schools of magic and gain extra Mana and Mana Regeneration per attribute point. +3 Intelligence, +2 Wisdom

Mages don't seem to get a class ability, but they get an extra magic school. I'm pretty sure they mean different types of magic rather than an actual school like Hogwarts. Being a spell slinger might be cool. If there is magic, shouldn't there be healing magic, or maybe nature magic like my Druid character in my husband's D&D campaign? I could swing being a Druid. Between our two bearded dragons, our three leopard geckos, ball python, and our dogs, I already have enough pets in the house to qualify. I should check out the rest before making my final decision.

Rogue: Rogues focus on stealth and on tasks best not seen in the light of day. Rogues can channel their mana into their stealth skills, rendering them nearly invisible instead of just trying to stay out of sight. Rogues receive 1 school of magic, class ability Fade, and gain extra Mana and Stamina per attribute point. +3 Agility, +2 Dexterity

Fade: Spend 20 Mana per minute to reduce your presence and make it more likely to avoid being noticed. Mana cost is halved when used in conjunction with Stealth skill.

Definitely not going rogue. I'm about as stealthy as a bull in a china shop.

Warrior: Warriors are the Combat specialists. They make up the front-line fighters, and ranged support. Warriors fill multiple combat roles in any party, depending on their attribute allocation and skill choices. Warriors receive 1 school of magic, class

> ability Bulwark, and gain extra health and stamina per attribute point. +1 to each physical attribute.

> **Bulwark**: Increase your defense for one minute by spending 10 Mana per extra point of defense.

Yeah, I'm not built for fighting. Nope, pain hurts, and I have no skill in any of the weapons John keeps in the house. I can barely shoot a bow in the right direction. All I know about swords is the pointy end goes in the other guy. Warrior is a definite pass. Looks like Mage is my best option. Rose made her selection, and the prompt disappeared.

A freezing pain coursed through Rose's body. Shards of ice seemed to cut through her flesh, so cold it seemed to burn, leaving behind a prickling numbness. Rose tried to cry out from the agony, but time still seemed frozen.

A ball of ice seemed to form just below her sternum. The pressure was intense as it grew, and it felt like it was pushing her organs aside. A deep cold radiated out of the ball of ice that made her very soul shiver.

It felt like an eternity before the blades of ice stopped slicing her up from the inside, and the sphere of liquid nitrogen stopped growing below her chest. Rose was begging internally for it all to just end. *Please let it be over. Let it be over, or just let me die. I don't care which right now.*

Slowly, the numbing pain seemed to ebb, replaced with gentle warmth. A warm sensation radiated out of that previously frozen ball. It flowed through the new veins where the ice had just torn her up from the inside.

> Path of Mana has been implemented. Mana Core has been created. Mana pathways established. Initial Mana Pool has been deposited in your Mana Core.
>
> Congratulations, the establishment of your Mana System repaired any deformities, injuries, or physical flaws.
>
> The initial deposit of Mana is consumed in the body restructuring process.

As a Mage, you receive 2 basic Magic School selections
Choose from the following list:

The next window that appeared looked like it had a few dozen options available to choose from. Each school of magic was organized by type. There were elemental magic schools like earth, air, fire, water, life, death, etc. Nature magic had beast and plant magics, there were also planar magics, Arcanum magics, whatever that meant, and a bunch more categories. Rose considered her options carefully.

When playing D&D with John and his friends, Rose always played as a druid. They were easy to play, and she always loved animals. It's what she knew best, plus druids usually had some healing abilities.

Since she wasn't sure about all the other schools of magic, Rose went with what she knew best and made her selection.

You have selected

Beast magic: Delve deeply into the nature of wild beasts. Form bonds with beasts, imbue yourself with their power or enhance their natural abilities.

Plant Magic: control the very plants around you. Heighten their potency; rapidly increase their growth and use them as extensions of your own will. You may even borrow their natural healing properties.

You may now select your Perk

Available perk choices are determined by analyzing the sapient receiving the perk, their surroundings, and the Path of Power chosen. Your available perk options are as follows.

Soul bound weapon: turn a weapon of your choice into a soul bound weapon. Soul-bound weapons cannon be lost or stolen unless the owner dies. Must choose a weapon on or near your person at the time of selecting this perk.

8

Convert beast to Bonded Familiar: change your pet or another nearby mundane animal into a Magical Familiar. Familiars are animals capable of leveling, but instead of having specific classes, a class archetype is chosen when bonded.

Class Related Magic Item: you will receive a class appropriate enchanted item or tool. This enchanted item will not be soul bound to you and thus may be lost or stolen.

I still don't know how to fight with a weapon, Soul-Bound or otherwise. So that one is off the table. Converting one of my pets to a familiar with its own levels and abilities sounds like a good option. It sounds better than an unknown magic item. If I chose Balder, he'll get stronger and help keep us safe. Yes, I think that's best.

You have chosen "Convert beast to Bonded Familiar" Target: Balder Husky/American Eskimo dog. Conversion initialized. ...

Choose Class Archetype
Mage
Warrior
Rogue

I'm already a mage type, and if I want Balder to protect us, I should choose the Warrior Archetype. That should give him the best chance.

You have Chosen: Warrior archetype...
...
Conversion Complete, you may view your Bonded Familiar's Status under the companion tab on your interface.
Good luck, Sapient. You are going to need it.

"MOTHER FUCKING SON OF A BITCH!" Rose screamed once she could move again. She was about to continue screaming obscenities until she heard the scream of pain and fear of a twelve-year-old boy behind her.

Rose spun around and saw her stepson Drake curled in the fetal position crying. She dropped the food dishes and rushed over to him.

"Drake, are you okay?" she asked as she wrapped him in her arms. As she comforted Drake, Rose noticed the sound of the water filter in the fish tank stopped flowing, and the only light in the living room was coming in through the window.

First these weird things, then we lose power? What the fuck is going on here? Rose thought.

Chapter 2

"I'm okay now, Rose. What's happening? God, that hurt a lot," Drake asked.

"I don't really know, dear. It's like something out of your father's books. There's no power, weird screens are popping up, some serious shit is about to go down. We need to get ready," Rose said.

A series of loud bangs came from outside, the squeal of metal twisting and deforming filled the air. A moment later, explosions went off in the not so far distance.

"What did you get? I'm a warrior now," Drake said with some excitement, the noise coming from outside barely seeming to distract him. "I got a Soul-Bound weapon to fight with." He held up an imaginary sword and swung it about. "Slay the monsters and level up. It's so cool."

"No, it's not cool. Frankly, it's terrifying." Rose stood up and had to catch her pants as they nearly fell to the ground. Her shirt also hung extremely loosely.

"Wow, Rose, you got skinny." Rake then looked down at himself and saw that nothing changed for him. "I guess I was already skinny, so I didn't change?"

"Stay here. I'm going to go grab a belt real quick." Rose went upstairs for a couple of minutes. She looked out the bedroom window, but unfortunately, it only showed the other townhomes in their complex. She couldn't see the street or anything further away. Smoke was filling the sky nearby, though.

When Rose came back downstairs, she heard a distinctive snap/hiss and low hum. *Oh no, what did that boy do?*

In Drake's hands, a silver and gold cylinder, one of John's custom lightsaber toys, emitted a black blade with a red aura around it. He was waving it around, making it hum.

"Rose, look, look. My Soul-Bound weapon is a lightsaber, well it says dark flame blade, but it's basically a lightsaber, right?" Drake said excitedly.

11

Rose looked around for a moment. "I don't think you can call it a Lightsaber. We don't want to be sued by Disney now, do we? Just call it your dark flame sword or something. Now, how do you turn it off?"

Drake pushed the button on the side of the hilt and the eerie blade sucked in, looking like the toy it once was again.

"Now what do you mean it said it was a dark flame blade?" Rose asked.

"Well, if you look at something really hard, a window pops up and tells you about it. Try it."

Rose stared at the hilt for some time before a blue-colored window appeared like the system message had.

Dark Flame Mana Blade (Soul-Bound)
Quality: Above Average
Rarity: Uncommon
Durability: 44/44
Damage: 16
Weight: 1.5lbs
Traits: Fire aligned Mana blade
Magic effects: Mana powered blade. Costs 10 mana per minute activated.
Power surge: Double mana expenditure for +50% damage increase
Mana pool: 100

Congratulations, you have gained the skill Identify. Identify rank 1.
You can now identify people, creatures, and objects by studying them for a moment. Increase your ranks to identify higher ranked opponents, items and to gain more details. +2% per rank to your ability to identify stronger people or items, +1% more information gained per rank.

Rose flicked the windows away when she heard a loud crash coming from the kitchen. She turned to look and saw the tail end of swirling lights as a creature manifested on her counter, knocking a dirty pot to the floor.

The creature looked like a cross between a chicken and a reptile. It had brightly colored feathers, short forelimbs ending in inch-long claws and stood on longer hind legs that seemed scaled and had almost two-inch claws on its feet. Instead of a beak, it had a scaled muzzle filled with tiny sharp teeth.

"WHAT THE FUCK?" Rose screamed and searched around her wildly. Balder began barking at the dinosaur-looking thing.

The creature screeched back at the dog

"It's a Compy," Drake exclaimed. "It's a real dinosaur. Can we keep it?"

Drake's exclamation snapped Rose out of her moment of panic, but leaving her slightly confused. "What? No, we can't keep a dinosaur. It's a wild animal that just appeared in our kitchen."

Balder bounded into the kitchen, his body language telling Rose he intended to play with it.

The Compy reared up to its full height, its nearly two-foot-long tail lashing back and forth. It screeched again at the approaching dog. "Balder! No!" Rose called. She did *not* want her dog to play with this dangerous creature.

Balder slid to a stop and looked back at Rose, confusion and disappointment on his face as he looked between his new toy and Rose. The Compy took that moment as its opportunity and jumped the nearly ten-feet that stretched between it and the fluffy dog. Arcs of electricity danced between its claws before it covered half the distance.

The Compy landed on Balder's back, its claws sunk in and the electricity singed his fur. Balder spasmed for a moment, let out a loud yelp, and tried to run away from the creature on his back. His paws scrambled so fast that he made no progress for a couple of seconds. Once he gained some traction, he bolted past Rose and Drake.

Rose lunged with her bare hands at the little dinosaur, not even thinking about what that thing's sharp teeth could do to her unprotected flesh.

While Rose hadn't managed to grab the Compy with her hands, she'd lunged too far, her forearm managed to smack the creature in its chest. Combined with Balder's speed; the Compy was effectively clotheslined and had been knocked off of the fleeing dog.

As the creature was scrambling to its feet, Rose heard that Snap/hiss again and Drake called out, "I got it!"

13

Before Rose could yell no, Drake made a wild swing at the recovering dinosaur. He wasn't accurate enough or quick enough to cut the creature in half like he'd obviously planned; instead, as the Compy darted away, he managed to shear off half of its long tail. It didn't just sever the tail of the Compy, the energy blade sliced cleanly through the couch and into the floor, leaving the couch smoldering from the heat of the blade.

The little dinosaur charged straight through the sliding glass back door, shattering it and lacerating its hide. That didn't stop the Compy; instead, it leaped over the six-foot wooden fence and disappeared from sight.

Once the Compy was gone, Rose shouted, "Get the fire extinguisher and put that out. !" Before rushing after Balder to tend to his wounds. Rose snatched up the first aid kit on her way upstairs. Balder was curled up against the bedroom door, whimpering.

Rose slowly approached Balder and gently stroked his head to help calm him. Once Balder was sufficiently calmed, she inspected the puncture wounds on his back. They looked deep, so Rose used a saline solution to rinse them out before applying some iodine ointment and wrapping the wounds up. She knew she should shave the area first, but with everything going on, this would have to do.

> Congratulations, you have gained the skill First Aid, First Aid Rank 6
> Using first aid, you can treat any number of injuries, reducing or stopping blood loss, increase health regeneration for a limited time, and reducing the duration of debuffs from injury. +12% health regeneration (2%/rank) for 8 hours after successful first aid treatment. -12% (2%/rank) duration to debuff resulting from injury. Reduces bleeding status by 100% if minor, 50% if moderate and 25% if major.

> Congratulations, you have gained the skill Animal Handling, Animal handling Rank 1
> You understand animal behavior and understand how to use that behavior to train and control animals. Animal handling helps tame and train animals faster and more effectively. +2% animal obedience, +1% training/taming speed

The skill gain prompts reminded Rose that she wasn't just a former medical assistant, she was a Mage now, and Mages have magic powers. Remembering how characters in John's books pulled up their character information, Rose focused on the word, Status. While still petting and comforting Balder, Rose looked over her character sheet first the first time.

Rose Baker
Mage Level 1

Str   11
Dex   11
Agi   12
Con   12
End   11
Int   14
Wis   14
Free attributes to spend: 3

Hp   60/60   Regen: 12/day
SP   110/110   Regen: 10/min
MP   196/196   Regen: 20/min

Perk: Soul-Bound Familiar

School of Magic
Beast
Nature
Skills
Beast Magic   Rank 1 (+2% effect, +1% resistance)
Nature Magic   Rank 1 (+2% effect, +1% resistance)
Animal handling   Rank 1 (+2% obedience, +1% training/taming speed)
First Aid   Rank 6 (+12% regen, -12% debuff timer)

Spells
Commune with beasts: Beast magic
Cost: 20   Damage: n/a   Range: self   Duration: 60 min   Area:
30 ft. Radius
Cast time: 5 seconds
Effect: Communicate mentally with any beast within 30 feet of the caster. Beast
understanding dependent on inherent intellect.
Tiger's Eye: Beast Magic
Cost: 50 Mana   Damage: N/A   Range: Touch   Duration: 60
minArea: n/a
Cast time: 5 sec
Effect: transform targets eyes into that of a feline. Gain low light vision, +30% to
notice movement, -15% visual acuity in well-lit areas.
Nature's Boon: Nature magic
Cost: 50 mana   Damage: n/a   Range: 30ft   Target: 1 Area:
n/a
Cast time: 5 seconds

Rose didn't really understand everything in her character sheet. She never considered herself a gamer, though she had played Dungeons and Dragons with John and his friends occasionally. With that bit of experience, she got the gist of what the stats and stuff meant.

Rose' stats were average across the board, except her mental scores, thanks to the bonuses she got from choosing Mage; her Intelligence and Wisdom were at fourteen each. With them being the primary stats for Mages, having them high was supposed to be a good thing. Just below the list of attributes, it showed her as having three unspent points. Without putting too much thought into it, she placed two into her Intelligence and one into her Wisdom.

With the extra points, her maximum mana pool increased by twenty-eight, and her mana regen increased by one per minute. Leaving her with a Mana pool of two hundred twenty-four and a Mana regen of twenty-one per minute.

Moving past that, Rose went straight to her available spells. She had two starting spells for each of the schools of magic she chose. For the beast magic, she had a spell to communicate with beasts and one called Tiger's Eye that literally transforms her eyes into that of a tiger's, granting low light vision.

The plant magic spells had what she needed right now. She had a root spell that could trap enemies, and she had a *healing* spell. Nature's Boon may only regenerate ten health over five minutes, but with Rose's health regeneration being only twelve per day, this spell was phenomenal.

Rose focused on the spell, trying to figure out how to cast it. As she did, information filled her mind. Strange symbols floated by her mind's eye and a tingly electric sensation moved from her chest, down her arm, and settled in her hand. Rose looked down and saw green lights shifting around her fingers until her entire hand glowed. It took about five seconds from start to finish. Once the light saturated her hand, she suddenly knew what to do next. She laid her hand on Balder's wound and the green energy flowed from her hand and into his body.

Focusing on Balder, Rose accidentally used the Identify skill and brought up his information.

Balder
Level 1
HP: 93/105

As Rose watched, Balder's health ticked up to ninety-four. Ten health over five minutes won't fully heal him, but another casting once it was done would bring him back to full.

Balder licked Rose's face once, letting her know he was feeling better already, and she rubbed behind his ears. Balder was a gentle animal and did an amazing job as her emotional support.

"Um… Rose? The fire is out now. Is Balder okay? And uh… the bearded dragons are growing?" Drake called up the stairs, getting Rose's attention. The last statement he made had the sound of a bewildered question.

Rose got back to her feet and went downstairs, Balder following at her heels. "What do you mean, the beardies are growing?"

"Uh… well… they are getting bigger. I mean, I see them getting bigger as I watch," Drake said.

Rose went to the terrariums John built to house their reptile pets. Drake was right; the bearded dragons were increasing in size right before her eyes. Their bodies were slightly bigger than her hand normally, with their hind legs resting over her wrist. Now they were as big as her forearm.

Rose hesitantly opened Krom's terrarium. She flinched slightly as Krom shifted his head to look at her. With a deep breath, Rose reached in and stroked his head and beard. He closed his eyes and relaxed into the touch. With a sigh of relief, Rose used Identify on the reptile.

Krom
Cultivation Rank 0

```
Hp: 25/25
Taming Progression: Genial 42%
Tamer: Rose Baker
```

"Huh, I guess I'm a beast tamer now," Rose said with a chuckle. She looked over to Alma and used Identify on her too.

```
Alma
Cultivation Rank 0
Hp: 25/25
Taming Progression: Friendly 52%
Tamer: Rose Baker
```

"I wonder if John will be annoyed that Krom considers me his owner instead of-" Rose was cut off as the sound of an aircraft flew fast and low, rattling the windows before there was a sudden tremor in the ground. The sound of shattering glass, breaking wood and tearing metal, louder than anything she had ever heard, assaulted her ears and nearly made the very air vibrate.

Rose ran to the front door, flung it open, and ran outside. A huge billowing plume of smoke rose over near Drake's old elementary school. Faint sounds of screaming could be heard. *With our technology no longer working...* Rose couldn't finish the thought. She looked over to the east, where the airport sat just a few miles away. Dread filled her as she considered all the planes that were in the air all over the world. *If they stopped working while flying, everyone in the air is probably going to die.*

"Drake, I know you're in the scouts. Grab what you need for an emergency real quick. We are going to your mom's house for now. There's safety in numbers." After giving her instructions, Rose went inside and gathered what she might need as well.

Chapter 3

Rose threw on her hoodie and grabbed a large backpack from the closet. She had to dump out all of John's gaming books before she went around to collect the necessities. She grabbed the large first aid kit from under the bathroom sink, then she dumped a box of granola bars in. Rose then grabbed a lighter from the junk drawer. John had always said that in a disaster, always have a way of making fire.

She couldn't think of anything else to grab at that moment. John's ex-wife—Drake's mother—only lived a few minutes away, maybe half a mile or so. *If we need anything else, I should be able to come back and get it easily enough.* Passing her gaze across the living room and kitchen, she saw the reptile terrariums. She couldn't leave them in there to starve. John had built the terrariums well, so that there was no chance of the lizards or his snake escaping.

Moving over to the lizards, Rose first opened up the doors for the leopard geckos. Luna was the easiest to extract. She was the friendliest and most outgoing of the trio. Rose simply had to place her hand in and Luna crawled onto it with no fuss. She slid Luna into the bug baggy pocket of her hoodie, then reached in to the other tanks and pulled out Toph and Katara. Toph was fairly easy as well. She suffered from enigma syndrome and didn't have the best coordination. Katara was the bitchy one. Rose had to trap her in the corner and gently pick her up. Katara tried to bite Rose on the thumb, but since she only had bony plates that were really only good for mashing up insects, it didn't even pinch.

After carefully stowing away the leopard geckos, Rose opened the tanks of Krom and Alma. She placed each on her shoulders, where they gripped with their sharp little claws and were happily secured. Finally, Rose pulled out Apophis, John's ball python. Despite the name, Apophis was a cuddly sweetheart and easily curled up into a ball in her hood. It was warm in there, so Rose was sure the snake would be just fine.

With all the reptiles secured, Rose looked around one last time and saw one of John's staves leaning against the wall in the corner. She snatched it up and then noticed the Damascus bowie knife and Kukri on the shelf next to where the staff had stood. Rose slid them onto her belt and gripped the staff in hand. She felt as ready as she could be to brave the chaos outside.

By the time Rose finished securing everything, Drake came running down the stairs wearing his scout's uniform. Rose had to stop her hand from smacking her own face. *I mentioned scouts and told him to get what he would need. Of course, he would take that as getting dressed for a meeting.* When he saw Rose standing there, bearded

19

dragons on her shoulders, knives on her belt and staff in hand, his eyes went wide. "I forgot Mufassa." He said, right before turning around and running back up the stairs.

Moments later, he had his own juvenile ball python wrapped around his left wrist. Rose also noticed Drake had the hilt of the lightsaber clipped to his own belt. She had a bad feeling about her stepson carrying around such a dangerous weapon, but with planes falling out of the sky and dinosaurs rampaging through her kitchen, she left it with him, but with a word of caution.

"Drake, you need to be extremely careful with that Mana blade. It is dangerous. I don't want you taking it out to play with or swing around all willy-nilly. It's like your father's gun. You don't play with that right."

"I know," Drake answered. A twelve-year-old's exasperation was obvious in his tone. "I'll be careful, and I won't treat it like a toy." Drake looked at the weapons on Rose again then said, "Are you going to get Dad's gun too?"

"I can't. your father has the only key to the safe, and I'm not that good with it yet, anyway. It's best to leave it where it is, safely locked away. You ready?"

"Yeah, I have my scout gear in my backpack. I have the rope, striker, knife, first aid kit, compass—"

"That's fine. You don't have to list everything. Come on, we are going now," Rose said, cutting off Drake's recitation. Rose grabbed Balder's thirty-foot extendable leash. Balder charged up to the front door, tail wagging ferociously and his whole-body wiggling in excitement. In his excitement, it was like he didn't even feel the cuts that hadn't healed yet. "Balder, sit!" Rose ordered, and he managed to obey after a moment. Rose clipped the leach onto his harness and they went outside once again.

Rose and Drake weren't the only ones going outside. Most of their neighbors who were home were making their way out of the townhouse complex to the street. They were all talking animatedly, stress lacing their voices. They kept pointing to the east and the south. When Rose turned to look where they were pointing, she noticed the massive pillar of smoke rising into the sky to the east. *That's over by the Airport. More planes must have crashed over there. All those poor people...*

An acrid taste tickled the back of her throat, making her cough. The smell of burning plastic and hot metal slowly thickened in the air as a haze of smoke blanketed the area. "Drake c-" Rose hacked out another cough before being able to continue. "Come on, let's get moving." Rose could see the fear in the boy's eyes as he nodded and followed behind her quietly, stroking his pet snake as he did so.

Crowds of people gathered in the middle of the street pointing all around, some vainly trying to get their cellphones to work. One group looked to be on the verge of exchanging blows as their heated voices echoed off of the nearby buildings. Rose avoided them all and kept moving towards her destination.

Rose maintained her determination to avoid the other people until the screams began. Turning her head, she saw a mass of what had been normal stray cats and dogs tearing into the helpless people. Some animals had been twisted nearly beyond recognition. "Oh, my God. What do I do?" Rose's heart thudded in sudden fear. Balder growled beside her and behind was that distinctive snap/hiss of Drake's Mana blade coming to life. Rose turned and saw a pair of rottweilers, each half again as big as the breed usually got and had metal-like spikes sticking out around their necks and down their spines.

Long ropes of foamy drool dripped from their snarling muzzles as they ran straight at Rose and Drake. Balder immediately interposed himself between the charging mutated dogs and his family. His normally white and fluffy coat darkened to a granite grey color and stiffened. His growl deepened and sounded like it came from a dog twice his size.

Drake moved up alongside Rose, his black bladed sword gripped so tightly in his hands that his knuckles were white, almost as pale as his frightened face. Before Rose could even think about what they should do, the mutant dogs were upon them, and Balder managed to jerk his leash out of Rose's numb fingers.

Balder intercepted the Rottweilers. He bowled right between them, knocking their shoulders with his own and making them stumble to the side. The spikes in their necks brushed up against Balder, but they didn't seem to penetrate his hardened fur. The two mutated dogs spun around and raced after Balder.

"NO, they are going to get him," Drake cried out. He let go of his Mana blade with his left hand and stretched it out. Over the course of two seconds, dark energy swirled around his hand and gathered into his palm. As soon as the energy condensed itself down to the size and shape of a golf ball, it launched from his hand and slammed into the backside of one of the mutant dogs. The animal let out a pained yelp and lost its balance as it was running. It fell and tumbled to the ground for a moment before scrabbling back to its feet, now glaring at the humans that had hurt it.

21

"Shit!" Rose swore. She almost berated Drake for drawing the creature's attention, but she remembered she had magic, too. As quickly as she could, she pulled up her spell list. She knew she had something that could help her, but couldn't quite remember what it was. Then she saw it, one of her nature magic spells. Following some strange, new instinct, Rose pointed the wooden staff in her hand at the beast and channeled her magic through it. Green light flowed down the length of the shaft and collected at its end. A couple of seconds later, the green light lanced out and struck the pavement beneath her target.

The beast slowly crept towards them, looking like it was getting ready to pounce. Right as it gathered itself for a lunge, the asphalt cracked under its paws and thin tendrils sprouted up. They grew rapidly and whipped themselves around the dog's legs and twinned itself around its torso. The monstrous dog growled and snapped at the roots, holding it in place, trying to free itself.

As soon as the dog was bound up, Rose saw Drake run forward with his blade held high. The boy was screaming incoherently. Rose tried to shout for him to stop, but the sounds couldn't get past the lump that had formed in her throat. Terror filled her heart as it tried to burst itself from her chest.

Rose head the Snarl from Balder and his opponent. Her eyes flickered over and she saw his teeth had changed. They had each elongated and taken on a hard-edged translucency that made her think of quartz. The crystal fangs easily tore through the flesh of the mutant dog, blood spraying over his stone-like coat. As Rose's gaze flicked back to the bound-up beast and saw Drake had already reached it. With a mighty swing, he swung his weapon like a little league bat.

After watching the Star Wars movies with John, Rose expected the blade to cut through the beast's neck with no resistance, but she was wrong. The blade seared the skin of the dog, but it did not pass cleanly through, it actually bounced off. The dog moved his head and snapped at Drake, and the boy could barely pull his arm away from the maw of the beast in time. While he managed to avoid getting bitten, he overcompensated and sent himself sprawling to the ground. The mana blade fell from his hand and skittered across the asphalt, the blade retracting as soon as it had left his hand.

Rose finally snapped herself out of the terror that had frozen her in place and rushed forward. The rottweiler was almost free, tearing away the roots with its teeth. *I have to end it before it gets free. Drake is still on the ground and helpless!* Rose pulled the Bowie knife from its sheath on her belt. As soon as she was in reach, she slammed the blade right in the middle of the creature's skull. The beast jerked hard to the side. A metallic *ping* sounded as the handle came away in Rose's hand, the blade remaining in the

22

animal's head. With a groan, the Mutated dog slumped down and rattled out its last breath.

```
Congratulations
Demon canine body rank 1 slain
You gain: 5xp
```

Rose dismissed the experience notification and looked at the now useless handle in her grip. *I thought Damascus blades were supposed to be really strong? John always went on how he wanted to make Damascus once he had his own forge.* Rose shook her head and dropped the useless piece of wood. She looked over at Balder. The mutated beast had its throat ripped out. Balder was limping his way back to Rose, his prey vanquished.

```
Congratulations
Demon canine body rank 1 slain
You gain: 5xp
```

Rose cast her Nature's Boon spell and Balder's health slowly started ticking up again. "Are you okay Drake?" she asked as Drake walked up to her. He'd collected his Mana blade and reattached it to the clip on his belt. He looked a bit disheveled, but no obvious wounds.

The sounds of screaming penetrated Rose's awareness. She looked back and saw everyone running in all directions. Dozens of people were on the ground, being savaged by the merciless monsters. Blood ran down the street in torrents, the coppery tang overwhelming the smell of burned plastics. Rose snatched up Balder's leash and grabbed Drake's hand. "Run!"

As they ran down the street, Rose noticed a teenager thrusting out his hand towards one of the mutated dogs. Red flickering light gathered in his hand, much like when Drake cast his dark spell. A ball of roiling fire launched from the teen's hand, but unfortunately the dog dodged to the side. As the dog lunged at the boy, tearing into the arm he raised to block, the boy's firebolt smashed into the side of a house. Instead of it harmlessly splashing off, the flame radiated outwards, and the building burned.

Rose rounded the corner with Drake. They were already over halfway to his mother's house.

Chapter 4

By the time Rose and Drake reached the house, they were both panting for breath and couldn't run any longer. Rose noticed one bar on her heads-up display was only at five percent remaining. When she focused on it, a tag appeared saying it was her Stamina bar. A moment later, numbers filled the green bar, showing she had six out of one hundred ten Stamina remaining. As she continued to walk up the driveway, she saw her Stamina slowly ticking back up.

Once they reached the front door, Rose opened the screen and pounded on the door with her fist. She hadn't even tried the doorbell, since there didn't seem to be any power anywhere.

After a couple minutes and several rounds of pounding on the locked door—she had tried the knob after the second round—, a woman's voice on the other side finally spoke up. "Who's there?"

"Kassandra, it's me, Rose. I have Drake with me," Rose answered.

"Rose? Drake? Oh my God, come in quickly. Thank God you're here," Kassandra said in relief as she unlocked both the doorknob and the deadbolt. Once the door had opened, Rose saw the five-four woman was pale as a ghost and had an alarming amount of blood covering her face and long brown hair. "You were a nurse or something before, right?" she asked, strain and near panic sending her tone much higher than it usually was.

"Medical assistant, why? What happened? Who was hurt?" Rose asked.

"It's Baron… his hand. It… it just blew up. Oh my god, there was so much blood," Kassandra cried.

Rose pushed Drake in and quickly followed, with Balder entering close on her heels. She held Kassandra for a moment, hoping to calm the distraught woman. "I can't promise much, but take me to him and I'll see what I can do to help." Rose released her and gently closed and re-locked the front door. It wasn't a lot of protection, but it was better than nothing.

Kassandra and Baron lived in a split-level home, with the kitchen and living room on the middle ground level, the bedrooms and a bathroom up a short flight of stairs and a den, small office and bathroom/laundry room downstairs. Kassandra took Rose down stairs after giving her son a fierce hug and a whispered, "I'm glad you're here and safe."

Down stairs, it was pretty dark. The windows had been covered with a dark cloth a long time ago, but the usual lights weren't working, instead a couple of oil lamps lit the space in their flickering light. Sitting on the couch, even more pale than Kassandra was, sat Baron. They had a belt cinched tightly around his wrist, acting as a tourniquet. His hand was mostly gone, what little remained was singed black.

"Hey… Ro—" hic, "Rose, how's it—" hic, "going." Baron's words were slurred and random hiccups interrupted his speech. Rose then noticed the large bottle of whiskey, mostly empty, sitting on the table in front of him.

"What happened?" Rose asked.

Baron waved vaguely with his good left hand and Kassandra answered as she came downstairs as well. "Some kind of… mutated rat came out of… out of, the crawlspace and tried to attack Kassie," Kassandra cried, tears streamed down her face as she recounted events not even an hour old. "Baron… he kicked the thing away at first and… and sent Kassie upstairs. It… it was all my fault. I grabbed Baron's gun. I was about to shoot-" she broke down crying in full force, not even able to finish what she had been saying.

"I took the gun from her and shhot the bashtard myshelf. Her hands shook, too musht. Wouldn't hit the broad shide of the barn. I winged the bugger, but my gun, it jusht, blew up in my hand." Baron finished with a wave of his seared stump.

"So, you got drunk to manage the pain?" Rose asked.

"Yesh, had nothing better than ib-ibu-ibuproflen… blah, you know what I'm shaying," He slurred.

Rose went over and examined the mangled stump, considering what she could do to help him. "I don't think it will heal cleanly as it is. I seem to have, well… magic now. And I can help it heal quicker. But we need to make it a clean cut, otherwise I don't know how it will turn out."

Kassandra managed to get a semblance of control over herself. Calm enough to talk, she asked, "A clean cut? You want to cut off what's left of his hand?"

"I think it's best. It's what doctors would do, I'm sure. It should heal over clean that way," Rose said.

Baron had a solemn look on his face as he considered what little remained of his hand. "Ish mostly gone already. Might ash well be done wish it," He said after a few long minutes of contemplation. "How ish we going to be doing it?" he asked.

Rose considered their options. *A really sharp cleaver or axe might do the trick, but it might also splinter the bone, making healing more problematic. A saw would be better, but it will be agonizing to saw through the wrist without anesthetic. There aren't any good options.* Rose then remembered Drake's Mana blade. *It was hot enough to cauterize the wound as it cut; it cut cleanly through her couch earlier, but it didn't penetrate the hide of the mutated dog all that well. But will it work well enough on non-mutated humans?*

"I have an idea, but we will need Drake's help," Rose said.

"Drake? Why drake?" Kassandra asked.

"After this whole Initialization thing, Drake turned John's lightsaber toy into the real thing. Or, at least this System's version of it. It calls it a Mana blade, and it's made of dark flame. It should be able to cut through cleanly and cauterize the would at the same time to stop blood loss. If we can do that, I can probably heal it in ten to twenty minutes," Rose said.

"That quickly? How is that possible? What do you mean, you can heal him?" Kassandra asked. Her voice began rising again. She seemed to be on the verge of freaking out again.

"Magic is real now. What Path did you choose when the world froze?" Rose asked.

"Wait, that was real? I thought it was some kind of mass hallucination," Kassandra said, momentarily shocked out of her rising hysterics.

"It was real. I chose the Path of Mana and became a Mage. I basically have nature magic. One spell I started with lets me heal five Health points over ten minutes. What did you guys choose?" Rose asked again.

"I... I chose the P-Path of Mana." Kassandra answered.

27

"What class did you pick? And what kind of magic?" Rose asked. She looked over at Baron and saw that he was distracted. He had tried to pick up the whisky bottle with his missing hand, swore, then awkwardly picked it up with his left before downing another swig.

"Oh, um… Rogue, I think? I don't really remember after everything. It all happened so fast," she said.

Rose considered it for a moment. "Have you checked your status screen yet?"

"Huh?" Kassandra looked really confused.

"Think hard the word Status and a window should pop up with all of your stats, class and everything," Rose instructed. Then she thought for a moment, then added, "Try to share it with me once you get it open."

Kassandra adopted a look of fierce concentration; it was that, or she was severely constipated. After a couple of long moments, she relaxed and her eyes opened wide in surprise. "It worked! Hmm… Share… Rose…" then a new window filled Rose's vision.

Kassandra Wulfson	
Rogue Level 1	
Str	11
Dex	14
Agi	15
Con	11
End	12
Int	11
Wis	11

Available Stat Points: 3

HP: 55/55	Regen: 11/day
SP: 168/168	Regen: 17/min
MP: 154/154	Regen: 15/min

Perk: Soul-Bound Familiar

Class ability:
Fade: 20 mana per minute to fade from everyone's notice. Mana cost is halved if

using a Stealth skill at the same time.

Magic school:
Dark Magic

Spells:
Shadow bolt
Cost: 40   Damage: 20   Range: 100ft   Duration: instant
Cast time: 2 seconds
Effect: summon a ball of condensed shadow and launch at your target.

Shadow step
Cost: 20 mana   Range: 120ft   Duration instant
Cast time: 1 second
Effect: step into one shadow and out another up to 120 feet away that you can see.

Skills
Dark Magic   Rank 1
Stealth   Rank 1

"So, you're a Rogue with dark magic. That's an interesting choice," Rose said.

"Well…" Kassandra said, blushing a bit in embarrassment. "I always played Rogues when we played D&D before. I didn't know it was real, and I just went with what was familiar."

"Speaking of familiar, which of your animals did you bond with? Or have you not chosen yet?" Rose asked.

Kassandra gave rose a blank look for a moment then asked, "What does a Familiar do? Is it like Dungeons and Dragons?"

"Well, I bonded Balder as my familiar. It seemed to boost his abilities, gave him magic of his own, and made him smarter. So it seems, anyway." Rose answered while fondly scratching Balder's head. He'd quietly come downstairs and laid down by her feet.

"Then I suppose I should pick Uni since she is my emotional support animal." Kassandra said, but then paused for a moment, tilting her head as though she were trying to hear something. Rose strained her ears and faintly picked out what sounded like a dog barking. "Uni! Oh my god, the dogs are still out back." Kassandra rushed up the stairs and to their back door. Rose could hear her call out. "Uni, Yoda! Oh no, it's got Yoda!"

Kassandra screamed out Yoda's name and rushed outside, without even a weapon in hand.

Balder looked at Rose, she looked back at him and said, "Go help, I'm right behind you." Rose then ran up the stairs behind balder, he had already started the transformation of his fur and fangs before he even reached the kitchen.

Once Rose reached the back door, she saw what'd happened. Yoda, a half Shepard and half husky who'd been getting a bit gray in the muzzle, stood between his mini-me and a mutated cat that was almost the size of a mountain lion. The big cat had Yoda pinned to the ground and was tearing into his belly with its claws. Blood and intestines were already spilling out, but Yoda wasn't just lying down and taking it. He had the cat's throat in his jaws and he was squeezing with every ounce of the fading strength he possessed. Uni stood hunched down, shaking like a leaf. The poor little Pomsky had her tail tucked between her legs and was whimpering in fear.

An errant thought passed through her mind at seeing the cat. Something *about John's audio books and a puma check? Or was it fecking pumas?* Rose shook her head and stepped outside. She saw Balder charge forward and crash into the huge cat like a rolling bolder. The cat tumbled to the side, but got quickly back to its feet. The two circled each other, lunging forward only to back away before the other could land a retaliatory strike.

Remembering that she was a Mage, Rose stretched out her hand and cast her only combat spell, Entangling Roots. As soon as the roots sprouted from the ground and touched the cat's paws, it leaped into the air with a spitting hiss. The cat managed to avoided the entanglement, but it worked as a distraction. Balder took advantage and grabbed the cat by the neck while it was still in midair. He sank his crystalline fangs in, deep. As soon as he landed, Balder shook his head vigorously until the dry, wood-snapping sound of bones breaking could be heard. The cat went limp and Rose got another experience notification.

Congratulations
Feral Domestic Cat Level 3 slain

You gain: 15xp

Rose rushed over to Yoda and tried to cast Nature's Boon on him, but the spell didn't take hold. Poor Yoda was still twitching, but when Rose remembered to use her Identify skill on him, she found out that his current Health points read zero.

"Poor guy. You were a good dog, fighting to protect your friend," Rose said, tears leaking out of her eyes. He wasn't her dog, but he was a good and friendly dog, well loved by his family. Wiping her eyes dry, she saw Kassandra crying as well while holding Uni in her arms, comforting the scared animal while drawing comfort for herself.

Rose cleared her throat. "We should get back in side, before something sees us."

Kassandra nodded and followed Rose and Balder inside, only to see Drake and Kassie's stricken faces. "What happened to Yoda? Is he... okay? He's got to be okay, right? You have... you have magic, you can heal him?" Drake asked.

It was apparent to Rose that the kids had seen what had gone on through their bedroom windows. Rose knelt down to be at eye level with the kids. She knew they'd lost pets before; their parents hadn't hidden death from them. But this would've been the first time they'd seen one of their pets die a violent death. Kassie, especially, would be deeply affected by it. She was only seven-years-old.

Rose had to swallow hard before she could speak. "I'm sorry. I don't have strong enough magic to save him. He was already dead before I could get to him and cast my spell. He was a brave dog, though. He saved Uni from the giant cat monster."

Kassie said nothing. She just quietly wept. Her mother set Uni down and picked up her little girl to comfort.

"I wish dad was here," Drake said with a sniffle.

Rose felt terrible. She had only been part of this odd extended family for a couple of years. She knew when they'd started dating that John was still on good terms with his ex-wife and that they had a child together. She did her best to not try to take the place of Drake's mother, but to still be there for him. It was a difficult balance to maintain, but Drake was worth it. She loved him like he was her own flesh and blood.

Rose never had kids of her own, was afraid to go off the medications that treated her bi-polar disorder, anxiety and other mental health problems she'd developed over her twenty-nine years. She was afraid to pass on her defective genes, with all the genetic disorders that ran in her family. While she'd always wanted a child of her own, she was too frightened of what she would give the child if she had one.

John didn't want to have any more children either, not after losing two of his sons already. Rose was content with that. If she couldn't be a mother herself, being a step-

31

mother, especially to such a kind and smart boy as Drake, was a good alternative. It was times like this though that she felt out of her depth, not having developed parenting skills as the child grew. But she did the best she could with what skills she possessed.

"I know, sweetie. I wish he were here too," Rose said before wrapping the boy in a tight embrace. The preteen resisted at first before giving in to the comfort and melted into her arms. "But knowing your father, I'm sure he is on his way here right this minute. Nothing can stop that stubborn man when he decides something needs done. And I know he will decide to be here. He'll stop at nothing to be by your side," Rose said.

"Where is he?" Drake asked.

"I talked to him just before this whole thing started. He was almost out of Idaho and into Utah," Rose answered. She knew she had to tell the truth to the boy. Lying or giving platitudes wouldn't help in the long nor in the short term. She had to keep it realistic, but with enough hope to keep him from despairing.

"How far away is that? When will he be home?" Drake asked, pressing for answers and, even if he didn't realize it, reassurance.

Rose thought about it, thinking back to when she and John team drove the truck together. "If I remember right, it's something like six or seven hundred miles away. I don't know how long it will take him, but know that your father will stop at nothing to be here. He will crash through any obstacle like a raging bull. Nothing can stop him." She gave him another big squeeze. "I need you to be brave though, okay? It's okay to be upset. The entire world has changed in an instant and it's very upsetting, not to mention terrifying, but we need to push forward. Right now, your step-father needs our help."

"What happened to Baron?" he asked.

"He tried shooting a monster with one of his handguns, but it blew up in his hand. I need to borrow your Mana blade so we can remove the damaged parts and heal the rest. Can I borrow it?"

"I don't know if it will work for you... it said it was Soul-Bound? And said something about no one else but me being able to use it," Drake said, uncertainty clear in his tone.

"Well, we can try it. If it doesn't work for me... well, we'll figure something out," Rose said.

Rose released Drake, and together they went downstairs, where everyone else had gathered. Rose really hoped that the Mana blade would work in her hand. She really didn't want to either put Drake through the trauma of cutting off his step-father's hand or put Baron through the trauma of trying to saw or hack it off. There were no good options.

Chapter 5

It was unfortunate, but Drake's Mana Blade wouldn't work for anyone else. While Kassandra and Rose discussed what they should do, Baron stood up. His drunkenness seemed to have passed at a rapid rate, and he had a hard and sober look in his eye. He picked up the inactive Mana Blade handle and turned to the boy.

Baron handed the handle to Drake. The boy looked confused as he took the weapon, and the confusion only grew when Baron wrapped his, much larger, hand around Drakes. "Close your eyes and turn on the blade. I will do it myself. This isn't your doing. I will control the weapon. You are not doing this, I am," Baron said. His tone was gentle, and he was clearly trying to reassure Drake.

"You're doing it?" Drake asked. He looked worried and stressed.

"Yes. You are not cutting me. I am cutting me. All you are doing is turning on the tool I am using," Baron reiterated.

"Um... okay," Drake said.

"Kassandra, take Kassie into the bathroom. She doesn't need to see this. Drake, close your eyes," Baron instructed.

Drake closed his eyes and swallowed hard.

"Turn it on," Baron told him.

With a snap/hiss, the black blade extended out of the hilt. The red aura-like glow from the blade lit up Baron's face, giving him a ghastly appearance. He tightened his jaw, and with a sizzling sound, brought his injured arm up and passed it through the blade in one quick motion. A dull meaty thud sounded as the rest of his hand, from the wrist up, hit the carpeted floor.

33

Baron released Drake's hand and dropped to his knees. A strangled, gurgling noise came from his throat as he fought back a scream of pain, his good hand clutched just below the cauterized stump and the smell of seared flesh filled the room.

"Oh my God," Kassandra cried out as she rushed from the bathroom to her husband. He wrapped her arms around Baron, her chest pressed against his back as she tried to give what comfort she could.

Rose rushed over a split second after, the glowing green light of her magic replacing the red glow of the Mana Blade as Drake shut it off.

Five seconds from when she'd started her spell, the green light flowed from her hands and suffused the seared wound. "That's the best I can do for now," Rose said.

"Daddy? Is daddy, okay?" Kassie asked as she stepped out. The little girl had one of her stuffed animals clutched in her tiny arms.

"Your dad is going to be okay, Kassie," Kassandra said gently to her daughter. She turned back to rose and asked, "Can you cast it again?" Kassandra asked.

"I... I don't know. But I can try," Rose answered. She started casting her spell again, and five seconds later she tried to heal Baron again, but the light only washed over his stump instead of sinking in like last time.

"It doesn't look like it will work. I can probably cast it again in five minutes, once the first one runs its course," Rose said. She bit her lower lip in concern. "Here, let's get him back to the couch. Let him rest while he recovers."

Rose and Kassandra helped lift Baron off of the floor and slowly guided his stumbling steps until he collapsed into the furniture.

"I... I'm so-sorry," Drake said, tears flowing down his cheeks as his gaze stayed locked on Baron's charred limb.

Rose moved over to Drake and spent some time comforting the child and reinforcing that it wasn't him, that Baron did it himself so that he would heal better. Rose had to stop comforting Drake twice to recast her spell, but by the time all three castings had run their course, Drake was calm and controlled again while Baron's stump was covered with a smooth cap of skin with no visible scaring.

34

Baron had passed out sometime between the second and third application of the healing spell. Everyone else had managed to settle down, though no one was actually relaxed. It was an eerie sensation, sitting quietly in a dimly lit room while echoing explosions, distant screams, and unholy shrieks filtered in through the walls.

Balder and Uni were laying together at the foot of the stairs, taking a nap in the relative quiet. Rose had taken the leopard geckos out of her hoodie pockets and placed them in a tote with a couple of hand warmers they'd found in the junk drawer. Apophis still lay curled up in her hood, soaking in Rose's body heat.

*   *   *

Sometime later, Kassie spoke up with a complaint. "I'm bored, and hungry"

"Here, have this as a snack," Rose said, while pulling out a granola bar from her backpack.

"Thank you," the cute girl said. Once she had the granola bar in hand, she looked at her mom and said, "I'm still bored. Can I play Minecraft?"

Kassandra let out a sigh. "I'm sorry, baby girl, but all the electronics are broken."

Kassie stomped her foot and declared, "I'm not a baby."

Drake groaned in exasperation. Rose knew from personal experience that having a sister four years younger than yourself could be trying. "Go color or something," he said, while fiddling with a Rubik's cube. He had been scrambling it, then solving it repeatedly.

Just as Kassie was about to open her mouth, clearly about to argue with her brother, their mother spoke up. "No fighting. Sorry, I know you're not a baby. And Drake, no telling your sister what to do. Kassie, why don't you play with your stuffies or color in one of your coloring books?"

"Fine," she said, drawing out the single word. Kassie then stomped her way into the playroom. The play room looked to have been meant for a home office or something, it wasn't much larger than the bathroom/laundry room and didn't have a closet, but it worked perfectly to hold most of the kids toys and give them a place to play without being in the middle of the living room.

Once Kassie was distracted, Rose moved over to Kassandra, who was sitting next to the sleeping Baron on the couch. "What are we going to do?"

"I don't know," Kassandra answered. "I don't even understand everything that's going on. I mean, we've all talked about what to do during a zombie apocalypse, or even a Mad Max kind of situation. But mutating animals? Magic? I don't know. I've always believed in magic. You know the burning candles, collecting crystals kind of thing, but you cast actual magic. You literally healed Baron's arm in less than twenty minutes. That should have taken doctors, surgery, and months of recovery." She flung her hands over her head in exasperation. Baron groaned in his sleep and shifted slightly before settling back down.

"You said you picked the Mana Path, right? You took the Rogue class?" Rose asked.

"Yeah, it was really weird. Everything froze and I couldn't do anything until I made my choices."

"I ended up picking Mage, and it got me two types of magic. I picked plant and animal. You chose dark magic right?" Rose asked.

"Yeah, since I picked Rogue, I figured dark magic would be the best fit. You know, sneaky sneaky, stabby stabby. It also gave me a special ability to go with the magic. What was it called again?" Kassandra sat there for a few moments wracking her brains trying to remember the name of the ability. She remembered that she could pull up her character screen, thinking *Status,* it popped up in her vision. After scrolling down a bit, she saw the ability she'd been trying to remember. "The ability is called Fade. It costs twenty mana-per-minute to use and lets me fade from notice, it says. Oh, and I have two spells. Shadow Bolt and Shadow Step."

"I know Shadow Bolt," Drake chimed in. He got up and moved over to where the two women were murmuring. He held out his hand and conjured up a tennis ball sized orb of darkness in his hand. "See, I have Dark magic too."

"Drake, Put that away. That's just as dangerous to hold as a gun. You know better." Rose snapped. She'd seen what that Shadow Bolt had done to those mutated dogs earlier.

"Sorry I-I didn't mean-" He replied and then glanced around, a bit of panic in his eyes. "What do I do? I don't know how to put it away." The black sphere quivered in his hand.

"Quickly, come with me." Kassandra said, and she bolted from the couch and went up the short flight of stairs to the back door. Drake followed, clutching his wrist with the unencumbered hand, trying to hold it steady. Once Kassandra had opened the back door, she turned and said, "Throw it outside."

Drake raised his hand and the moment it pointed outside, the bolt shot away at an angle into the sky. Once it traveled about a hundred feet, the sphere detonated in a burst of darkness that quickly faded away.

"Don't do that again. This isn't a toy, it's dangerous," Kassandra scolded.

Drake's eyes were red and his lips quivered as he did his best to fight back against the tears that slowly leaked out.

Kassandra felt bad from lashing out in her fear. She enveloped her son in her arms and held him as sobs burst forth and his skinny frame shuddered. Once his crying subsided, they went back downstairs.

Kassandra let Rose distract Drake after coming back down stairs, telling them more about her abilities. "I have four starting spells, two each for my Plant and Beast magic. I have that healing spell, Natures Boon, that can heal ten Health over five minutes, and my other nature spell is simply called Root. It makes roots spring up and entangle monsters."

"That's pretty handy," Kassandra said. She remembered a similar spell from D&D and knew it was a pain in the ass to deal with.

"It helped us get here. When we were attacked by the mutant dogs, it trapped one of them. My Beast magic spells aren't as directly useful, though. At least going by their descriptions. Tiger's Eye is supposed to transform my eyes into actual tiger eyes, and is supposed to give me night vision. The other one is interesting though, it's Commune with Beasts. If I cast it, I'm supposed to hear the thoughts of animals around me and they can understand mine."

"Have you tried them yet?" Kassandra asked.

"No, not yet. So far, I've only cast the Plant magic spells. I could try them, though." Rose said.

"They don't seem destructive, so why don't you give them a shot?" Kassandra said.

"Yeah, I think it'd be cool," Drake said. His eyes were still red and puffy, but he seemed past being upset.

"Ok, let's try Eye of the Tiger," Rose declared.

"The thrill of the fight," Kassandra muttered. she tried but couldn't suppress her smile at the joke.

Rose simply rolled her eyes before focusing on the spell. Kassandra watched as the magic built up in Rose's hands for five long seconds, then Rose reached up and touched her closed eyes and the amber colored light flowed off of her fingers and passed through Rose's eyelids.

When Rose opened her eyes, Kassandra saw that they had turned a yellowish-gold color and her pupils had elongated like a cats.

"Woah, that's weird," Drake said. "Your eyes turned yellow."

"I've got to see this," Rose said just before standing up, but a bout of vertigo seemed to wash over her and she swayed. Rose closed her eyes for a minute and seemed to steady herself before trying again. Taking careful steps, Rose made her way to the bathroom and saw the glowing eyes of a predator looking back.

Rose staggered back, a scream tearing from her throat.

"What the fuck!" Baron yelled as he launched himself off of the couch, Rose's scream clearly having woken him up. He was spinning around, looking for danger, while Kassandra leaped to her feet, staring into the bathroom.

"Sorry, everyone, calm down," Rose said, her cheeks flushing in embarrassment. "I thought I saw something, but it was just my reflection."

It was then that Baron looked at her face. "What the fuck happened to your eyes?"

Rose then explained to Baron about how they were trying out their new magic and what they were discussing while he had slept.

"Well, I don't have any special abilities like that," Baron said. He took a deep breath and then froze. His eyes unfocused and it looked like he was watching something nobody else could see.

"Baron? Are you okay?" Kassandra asked.

He held up his stump, realized what he had done, and then said, "Just a moment. I've got some kind of tutorial video playing."

A few minutes later, he blinked. "Well, that was some strange kind of bullshit. At least they could have done better animation."

"What?" Kassandra asked.

"Apparently, I breathed in this Essence stuff for the first time, so this System thingy showed me the basics of how to turn it into Ki. It's what I'm supposed to use instead of Mana. Damn it, I should have just picked the Path of Mana like you all did. It would be simpler than this shit. Now I've got to meditate to make this stuff, then open these Meridian things. You can just level up to get stronger."

After some more discussion about their different advancement options and what abilities they had or might create, in Baron's case, they brought their discussion around to more immediate matters. "So, what do we do?" Rose asked the same question that started that whole discussion.

"Let's give it until morning. We should wait and see if the power comes back on and if the phones start working again. I also think we should all sleep down here tonight, just in case. I should go to the garage before it gets dark out, though. We can use the fireplace to make dinner, but all of our camping supplies are out there. If everything works again, I don't want to ruin our pots or pans by sticking them in a fire."

"Fuck the pots and pans. There are damn monsters out there. If things go back to normal, we can buy new pots and pans. I don't want you going out there and getting attacked." Kassandra said. The scene of Yoda being disemboweled by the huge cat replayed in her mind and she shuddered at the thought of something doing that to her husband.

"Fine, whatever. I think we should hunker down. I wouldn't be surprised if the Governor declares martial law. We have three military bases and the air force academy here. Between them and the police, they should get a handle on all this shit before too long.

39

We have enough nonperishables to last quite a while, and we can eat the stuff that can spoil first."

"What about water? If the power outage isn't just our neighborhood, how long will the water last?" Kassandra asked.

Baron brought his stump up to the side of his head, as though he had been trying to scratch. When the stump hit his head instead of his fingers, he grimaced at it and switched to his off-hand. "I don't know if the power outage is just around here or city wide. None of the radios are working, not even the battery-operated ones." Baron sighed before continuing, "Just in case, we should collect as much water as we can. If the power outage is widespread, the water pressure could drop at any time over the next couple days, if not sooner."

"What if one of those monsters gets in here?" Kassandra asked, her gaze shifting to the recent bloodstains.

Baron stood up and walked to the wall, where he had a few things hanging. He pulled down a sheathed weapon. It had a stylized handle with a twenty-inch blade. It looked like a stretched-out Bowie but with a more fantasy style to it. He gripped the sheath in the crook of his elbow and pulled out the blade with his left hand. "Then we deal with them," He said.

"If I'd remembered that I could've chosen a Soul-Bound weapon, I might not have lost my hand." Baron said as he stared intensely at his favorite blade. He turned his head and answered his wife's last question. "If we get attacked, then I'm putting whatever dares to attack us down, *hard*."

Baron twisted his head and stared at the knife in his hand. In his grip, the light reflecting off of the large, single-edged blade seemed to shift. It took on reddish streaks before silvery drops formed from its tip. As though they were watching a time-lapsed video of ice melting, more drops quickly formed and flowed down the weapon until it became a puddle of liquid steel in his hand.

Looking more like mercury than steel, the weird material stretched out like some kind of sci-fi horror, touched the end of his right arm, and then transferred itself over to the other limb completely. The metal covered the stub of his arm like a sock, before extending out from its center.

A few seconds later, the steel re-solidified into a foot and a half single-edged recurved blade. It had a flowing, Damascus-like pattern that almost looked like flames etched in a faintly glowing red. It looked as though the heat of a forge radiated out of its lines.

The blade was now firmly affixed to Baron's arm, with a steel cup that was perfectly melded with his actual flesh. There didn't seem to me a seam or anything between the metal and skin, it just seemed to simply flow from one material to the other.

Kassandra stared at the weapon so long that a window popped up in front of her.

Solblade (Soul-Bound)
Quality: Above Average (+10%)
Rarity: uncommon
Durability: 40/40
Damage: 20
Weight: 1.5 lbs.
Ki effects: Ki pool regenerates at 1 point per 10 minutes. Infuse Ki into the blade to deal fire damage. Infuse 10 points of Ki to extend blade to 3 feet for 5 minutes dealing an extra 10 base damage.

"Well, damn. That's unexpected." Baron said, as he looked on in confusion. He twisted his arm one way, then the other, watching how the cup conformed and moved with his arm. "This feels weird as fuck. You're all seeing this, right? I'm not hallucinating?"

"N-No, I'm seeing it too," Rose and Kassandra both said almost simultaneously, not the same words exactly, but the meaning was the same. They'd all seen some crazy things that day. Insane things like mutated animals, planes falling from the sky, and even magic spells that could heal almost anything in mere minutes. But this, this really pegged everyone's what-the-fuck-ometer.

Chapter 6

Once everyone had calmed down; Baron, Rose and Kassandra got to work securing their home and collecting water. Rose and Kassandra pulled out every container that could hold water and filled them. They also plugged up the bathtub and filled it with water as well, while Baron quietly stepped out the front door with Drake.

The side door to the garage was immediately to the left of their front door and they managed to unlock it and go inside before they caught any monster's attention. With the help of Drake, Baron collected several sheets of plywood they'd planned on using to make a shed out back, along with several wood boards, nails, and the tools they'd need to block off the windows.

It took several hours, and a lot of swearing from Baron as he tried to adapt to only using his left hand, but with Drake acting as a spare set of hands, they managed to cover up all the ground-floor windows in the house.

With the house buttoned up tightly and everyone staying as quiet as possible, two days slowly passed. It was fairly quiet in the house, when the shrieks and roars of monsters fighting or the screams of people in pain didn't send everyone's hearts pounding in fear. Baron spent his time trying to master meditation and cultivation. Rose and Kassandra spent their time entertaining Kassie and Drake and doing their best to keep everyone's spirits up. In that time, they also explored some of their less destructive abilities, learning as much as they could about this new System as they could.

Half way through the third day of living in the dark, Rose was boiling water to make ramen for everyone to eat for lunch. Her heart leapt into her throat when there was sudden, loud pounding on the front door.

Baron leaped to his feet and practically flew up the stairs, arriving quickly at the front door. Kassandra used her Rogue ability, Fade. Rose assumed she was following behind Baron to provide backup. Rose decided to stay downstairs with the children and the pets, preparing to be the last line of defense, if necessary.

"Thank god, I saw the smoke from your chimney and hoped there were more survivors here." Rose heard an unknown man's voice filter down stairs. Rose made her way to the stairs so she could hear better.

"What's going on out there?" Baron asked. He looked out past the man, scanning for monsters. "Wait, come in side, we don't want to attract attention." Baron pulled the man inside, then quickly shut the door.

"There are monsters everywhere..." The man trailed off when he noticed the bare blade where Baron's hand should have been. He shook his head for a moment before continuing on. "So many people have died, and the government is nowhere to be seen. Right now, we're directing survivors to the elementary school just over there. You know, safety in numbers," The man said, pointing to the west. "We are also collecting supplies from the neighborhood."

"Does anyone know what's actually going on?" Baron asked.

"No one knows a damned thing. It seems like everyone has a theory. Some say it's Judgment Day, some think Alien invasion. Hell, some nerds were even talking about some book series, System Apocalypse I think it was? By some Canadian author with an Asian sounding name. Tow Wang, Chow Wong, something like that. All we know is that we need to get together and protect ourselves. It's not just mutated animals out there anymore, there are some straight up Lord of the Rings, Harry Potter type monsters out there."

Baron had a worried look on his face. "I don't know. We seem fairly safe here. We've been keeping real quiet and nothing seems to bother us."

The man shrugged. "Stay. We aren't forcing anyone to gather, just letting you know where we are. You've been lucky so far. Several houses have holes smashed through the walls. Others collapsed. So much blood splattered all over the damned place." He gestured at the plywood covered windows and the walls. "Nothing seems to stop them if they catch your scent. They break right through plywood walls. The school is made of cinderblocks, and all the windows are boarded up with metal tables. Working together, those of us that can fight back have been able to repel the monsters. Anyway, you know where the school is if you choose to join us. I need to get back out there and find more people."

"How are you able to go out there and not get killed by the monsters?" Baron asked. He didn't see any obvious weapons on the man, and even though his clothes were dirty, they didn't seem to be torn up.

The man smiled and lifted his hand. An orb of fire formed there and floated just above his palm. "I'm a level three Mage. Between my Fire and my Earth magic, I can stop most of the more common monsters around here." The fire winked out as he closed his fist.

43

"Look, I've really got to move on. There's a lot of homes on this street I still need to check on."

The man turned around, cracked the door just enough to peek out and make sure the way was clear. Once he was satisfied, he opened it wider and slipped out, closing it quietly behind himself.

Kassandra dropped her Fade ability and looked at Baron. "Do you think we should go? The water has already stopped running. We don't have a lot of wood left to cook with. What are we going to do?"

"Let's go back downstairs, and we can talk it over," Baron said.

Once everyone settled in, Drake joined them while Kassie stayed in the playroom, coloring.

"I don't like the idea of taking the kids out there. We could have died just coming over here," Rose said, starting them off.

"I don't like it either," Kassandra said. "But how long can we stay here?"

"Between the jugs, pots, and the bathtub we filled, we should have enough water to get by for four or five more days. But that doesn't include using it to cook with. Pasta, rice and most of our dried goods need water to prepare. The canned stuff we've got won't need any, though. Normally I'd say we had close to a month's worth of food in the house, but without electricity, our chest freezer is already mostly thawed."

"So maybe three or four days if we use water to cook with," Rose summarized.

"What do we do then?" Drake asked.

Baron got up and started pacing. He almost stabbed himself in the head as he tried to run his non-existing fingers through his hair. He switched to his left hand, swearing under his breath. "I don't know. I know we can't stay in here forever. But it's dangerous out there, but nothing says monsters won't make their way in here." Baron groaned in frustration. "It's a damned if you do damned if you don't kind of situation."

The conversation went on in circles for a while, but they couldn't come up with a suitable answer. After deciding on a wait and see approach, they'd settled in for another long, hard day of remaining unnoticed.

Early the next morning, while holding a lit candle for illumination and a roll of toilet paper, Rose opened the door to the under-stairs closet. in the back of the closet was a two-foot square panel that lead into the houses crawlspace. Since they didn't want to risk the dogs getting attacked, and didn't want them relieving themselves in the house proper, they'd been letting them do their business in the dirt. Since the water stopped running, the people in the house were forced to use it as a bathroom as well.

After Rose opened the access panel, she paused and listened hard. She'd thought that she'd heard something, but after a moment, it was quiet. Rose extended the candle to illuminate as much as she could, but the light it cast didn't extend very far.

Wait, there it is again, She thought as she picked up the faint noise. It sounded like something with claws was scratching. Concerned about a monster making its way under the house, she cast her Tiger's Eye spell. As soon as it was complete, the shadows seemed to retreat, and she could make out more.

Balder nudged himself past her legs, head poking through the opening, and let out a low rumble of a growl.

In the back corner, far away from the main part of the house they stayed in, something was digging around the hole they used for a latrine. The moment it heard the menacing growl coming from Balder, the creature stopped and turned to face them.

It was a ghastly-looking creature. It had the body of a cat, maybe two-feet-long, but it had a slimy octopus-like head with a bunch of squirming tentacles writhing around.

Cephiline
Level 5
HP: 75/75

Rose stared long enough for her Identify skill to trigger, which helped break her from her almost trance-like state. "Shit! Monster under the house," she yelled back into the room, her full bladder forgotten.

The monstrosity flared its tentacles wide, screeching at Rose and revealing a large, beaked mouth at its center. A second, similar sounding, screech came from the hole, followed closely by a third. As the first one advanced on Rose and Balder, Rose saw wriggling tentacles protruding from the hole. More were coming in!

Balder dashed in, launching himself at the advancing monster. Baron came stumbling in to the closet while shouting, "Clear the way!"

Rose quickly ducked into the crawlspace. Even her five-foot-three-inch body had to duck in order to fit. As soon as she was out of the way, she cast her Root spell to slow down the monsters climbing out of the hole. The thick brown goop that clung to the monsters' bodies intensified the odor of human waste, nearly making Rose gag. But she swallowed hard and focused on completing her spell.

The second cat-octopus creature managed to fully extract itself from the hole and the third had just crested the edge when the spell went off. The woody tendrils began wrapping around each beast

Balder wasn't doing well against the mass of tentacles. He'd already triggered his stone fur ability, so he wasn't taking any damage yet, but the first monster already had Balder's head wrapped in its limbs and was trying to drag the poor dog closer to its vicious looking beak.

Scrambling on his knees and his one good hand, Baron quickly shuffled into range. His Soul-Bound blade glowed a dull read and radiated waves of heat. The steel hissed as he rammed the weapon into the side of the cat-like beast. It let out a louder shriek than before and it's tentacles released Balder from their grip as they spasmed.

Balder snapped at the creature with his crystalline fangs and had managed to shear off one of its tentacles. Dark, almost black, blood sprayed from its stump as it tried to pull away. Unfortunately for it, Baron brought his good hand into play. He managed to grab it from behind the head, ripped out his now smoking knife, then slammed it into the bulbous, sack-like head. With a viscous twist, he ripped the blade sideways and cut a huge gash. Sickly looking ichor and other tissues splashed out. The smell of it made the shit stink seem like roses in comparison.

Orbs of pure darkness struck the entangled monsters. Rose turned and noticed Kassandra in the entryway, lobbing a new Dark Bolt every two seconds. Behind her, giving off that weird red glow from a black blade, stood Drake. "Come on mom, I can help," He whined.

"Get back and protect your sister," Kassandra ordered.

Seeing the resolute face of his mother as she turned back to launch another Dark Bolt, he sighed and left the closet, scuffing his feet on the carpet as he went.

It didn't take too long after that to finish the remaining two monsters, just awkward. Fighting in a room with a ceiling less than four-feet-tall sucked.

Once it was over, the bodies looted and Rose's healing spell cast on Baron to help with a couple of minor injuries; they sat in the downstairs living room once again. "Okay," Baron said. "I think we should go to the school. Things are making their way into the house, and I don't have the means to make it more secure."

He didn't receive any arguments, and they fell into a discussion about logistics and the best way to get there safely.

Chapter 7

After packing up as many supplies as they could reasonably carry, the adults equipped themselves with what weapons they had available. Besides Baron's Soul-Bound blade, he grabbed one of his hatchets and, with Kassandra's help, threaded the leather loop on his left side so he could easily draw it with his good hand.

Kassandra belted on a twelve-inch Bowie and a seven-inch K-Bar. she kept one of their other hatchets in her right hand and Kassie's tiny hand clasped in her left. Rose stuck with John's staff she brought with her and the Kukri she'd brought from home. She also picked up a spare Bowie knife Baron had. Rose shook her head as she remembered a time she'd teased John about how many knives he'd owned. Never again would she make fun of someone for having so many weapons on hand.

Drake already had his Scout survival kit and had his Mana Blade attached to his hip, where he could reach it quickly. The only one that wasn't armed was little Kassie, being only seven-years old. She'd had no knife handling training, aside from butter knives, so her parents decided it would be safer for her to not carry one.

Rose had the reptiles secured in and on her hoodie once again. Balder and Uni were leashed and ready to go. Baron was about to open the front door when he paused and turned to look at Kassandra. "I just had a thought. I know we wanted to wait until we learned more about what was going on before assigning Kassie's Perk, but if we are going out there, I think we should give her every chance we can, in case something happens. What were the options again?" he asked.

Kassandra thought about it for a moment before answering. "You're right. Everyone else has used their Perk. Give me just a moment." With a deep breath and that strange unfocusing of her eyes, Rose watched as Kassandra brought up her interface and found the section she was looking for. "The options are: double Health Regeneration, double Stamina pool, or double Stamina Regeneration."

Baron thought about the options for a moment. "If anything happens to us, her best chance at survival will be to run away as fast as she can. While increasing her stamina regeneration will help her recover faster, I think it would be better for her to run for twice as long at full speed. The school isn't that far away, so if we double her Stamina pool, she should be able to make it there in a single full sprint. What do you think?"

Kassandra nodded her head. "With her not having the option to choose a Path for another year, and circumstances being what they are, I don't see a better option." She had tears in her eyes as she poked her finger at the option only she could see.

Kassie shivered for a moment as the Perk took effect. Once it was over, her eyes shone and she practically vibrated in her shoes. It looked like the little girl had taken a hit of pure caffeine and couldn't hold herself still.

Baron kneeled in front of his daughter and looked her in the eyes. "Kassie, I want you to listen to me carefully. Are you listening?"

She bobbed her head quickly in the affirmative, now bouncing on the balls of her feet.

"Pay close attention, okay? We are going to your school. It might be dangerous out there; monsters might try to get us. Do you understand?"

"Like what got Yoda?" Kassie asked. She slowly stopped bouncing and acting hyper after she mentioned their dog. Now she stood there, eyes glistening with unshed tears, listening to her father.

"Yes, monsters like what got Yoda. And other kinds might be out there too. We are going to your school where other people are gathering. It's going to be safer there than it is here. But it will not be safe getting there. Do you understand?"

Kassie clutched her unicorn stuffy close to her chest as she nodded her understanding.

"I want you to make me a promise. I want both of you to make me a promise," Baron said and looked at Drake. "If anything happens to me, your mom, and Rose, you run as fast as you can to your school. Get to the grownups there. Drake, if something happens to us-" Baron's voice caught for a moment. After clearing his throat, he continued. "If something happens to us, I need you to promise me you will look after and protect your sister. You're too young for a responsibility like this, but if something happens to us, you are the only one we can trust to take care of her. Understand?"

"But I don't—" Kasie said before Baron cut her off.

"I need you to promise me, if something happens to us grownups, you will run to your school as fast as your little feet can carry you." Kassie opened her mouth to object again, but Baron beat her to it. "Promise me."

Tears fell from her eyes and her head hung low, but she nodded her head and mumbled, "I promise."

"Good. Drake?" Baron said as he met his stepson's eyes.

Drake's eyes were wet with tears as well, but after a dry swallow, he stood up straighter and nodded firmly. "I promise," he said.

"Okay," Baron said as he stood back up. Slowly, Baron opened the door a crack and looked outside. After a few moments, he carefully opened the door the rest of the way and stepped outside. One by one, everyone followed him out. The morning sky was a hazy red, the sun could barely be seen behind the thick layer of smoke that seemed to cover the entire world.

Blood smears, old and fresh, decorated the street and sidewalks. Fortunately for the kids, though, there were no corpses in sight. An eerie silence filled the air. It was so quiet, Rose's ears rang. In her entire adult life, Rose had never experienced this complete lack of sound. Its very absence made her itch and twitch.

Their group moved slowly and quietly down their side street. Normally, they would have been able to see the school from the end of their driveway, but with all the smoke filling the air, they couldn't even see the end of their road clearly.

It took the group nearly five minutes to reach the end of their street, peering under every parked car and into every bush. One might think that the lack of any monster jumping out to attack them would reduce their stress, but one would be wrong. With each house they passed, the tension had grown. It hadn't taken long before their breath became ragged, the threat of panic rising with each step.

Rose's heart thudded painfully in her chest. She kept Balder's leash short in her tight grip, not wanting him to wander about like he usually did on their walks. He clearly wanted to, nose twitching at every blood stain and bush. Rose knew he wanted to explore every unfamiliar scent he came across.

Now that they made it to the intersecting road, all they had to do was cross the enormous field that stood between them and the elementary school. They could just make out the building through the haze. After observing the field for a bit and not seeing any movement, they crossed the street and slowly stepped onto the grass.

"Well, that was anti-climactic," Baron muttered as they reached the school parking lot. No monsters jumped out at them from the knee-high grass nor did anything dive bomb them out of the sky.

50

"Who's there?" a male voice called out in that weird half shout, half whisper people use when they need to be heard at a bit of a distance, but feared being overheard.

Baron spun around while brandishing the bare blade attached to his wrist. Kassandra nearly jumped out of her own skin. Rose brought her hand to her chest, feeling as though she might have suffered a micro heart attack. Kassie let out a small scream and Drake fumbled at his waist for his Mana blade.

It took everyone a moment to locate where the voice had come from, but they eventually noticed the figure of a man on top of the school roof.

"Don't scare us like that," Baron growled. "We were told that you were gathering people for safety."

"Thank God, more survivors. Come around to the front of the school, all the side doors are barricaded. I'll have someone open the door to let you in." The man then moved away from the edge of the roof and disappeared out of their sight.

Following his directions, they went to the main entrance of the school. One of the metal front doors was slightly ajar when they rounded the corner. As soon as whoever stood behind it saw the group approach, the door opened the rest of the way.

What looked like a police officer stepped out. He was wearing a bullet-proof vest and a black uniform that'd seen better days. He looked to be in his mid-twenties. "Come in quickly. It's clear for now," he said, while gesturing for everyone to come inside. In his other hand, he held his nine-millimeter service pistol.

Obeying his instructions, they all went inside and the cop closed the door behind them and bolted it closed. Someone had bolted on a pair of brackets and used a heavy metal pipe at a functional bolt to lock the doors. The school used to use electronic locks that the office staff could buzz people in.

Once safely inside, Baron looked at the man and while holding up his missing hand. "What the hell are you doing with that thing? You're going to blow your damned hand off if you use it." He said in a hard tone.

"It's okay sir. I can imagine what you've been through. Several other people have been seriously injured trying to use a firearm. This is my Soul-Bound weapon. I'm not sure exactly how it works, besides magic. But it is safe for me to use. It even creates its own ammunition," the officer said.

Using the Identify skill he picked up from Rose, Baron pulled up the policeman's information.

| Carl Bronson |
| Warrior Level 4 |

"Let's get you settled in and some water to drink," Carl offered.

"You guys still have water?" Kassandra asked, past the rasp in her throat. Her throat was sore and dry from the smoke and stress.

"We got lucky. One of the Mage types has access to water magic. He's been spending most of his waking time filling containers with clean water to drink. If you get some right after he conjures it, it's pleasantly cool too. I'm sure you have a lot of other questions, but I need to keep guarding the door. Margret, the principal here, has been organizing everything and will be more than happy to see you to where you'll be staying. She'll be the one to answer your questions. It's not fancy, or very comfortable, but it's safe. You're safe here," Carl said. He was clearly trying to reassure the family, though a slight shift of his eyes to the side told them he wasn't entirely sure he believed it himself.

Chapter 8

"Hello, my name is Margret. I'm the... I was the principal here before... well, everything," Margret said with a vague hand waving gesture. She was an older woman, probably in her mid to late fifties and had her, more gray than brown, hair wrapped up in a messy bun. She looked tired, puffy bags lined her eyes, and they didn't seem to fully focus on any one person. "We've converted most of the classrooms into living areas for everyone taking shelter with us. It's not the most comfortable, or private, but it's better than the alternative."

"Marge, are you ok?" Kassandra asked. She'd noticed that the principal hadn't seemed to recognize them, even though she was the presiding principal for both Drake when he went there and Kassie. Kassandra'd volunteered to help at the school many times and had spoken with Margret often enough.

"Marge?" Margret replied, the question clear in her tone. She focused her tired eyes on the people standing before her. It took a moment, but Kassandra saw the light of recognition kindle when the principal realized who had arrived. "Oh my God, I'm so sorry," She said while shaking her head. "Everything's been so crazy and frankly, exhausting. I'm so glad you all survived."

Margret wrapped Kassandra in a hug for a moment before turning to Drake and Kassie and warmly embraced the children together. Kassandra saw the tears trailing down her face while she held the children. Baron and Rose stood there awkwardly for a few moments until Balder walked up, snuffled at her face before giving her a single lick.

"Oh my, I'm... I'm so sorry. I must look terrible," Margret said as she stood back up and surreptitiously wiped away her tears. "Here, come with me. Unfortunately, we don't have any vacant classrooms for you to stay in. We're housing two or three families per room right now." The principal said as she guided everyone down one hall to the room they'd be staying in.

"We've repurposed the gym mats so everyone will have something to sleep on. We are still short on blankets and pillows, but our scavenging teams are bringing more in everyday along with much needed supplies and any survivors that are willing to join us."

"How is everyone holding up? " Rose asked.

Margret let out a long sigh. "Some are holding up better than others. Frankly, I'm surprised at how many people, especially the younger ones, are adapting to everything.

But the others... I wish we had better options to provide counseling. Many are showing signs of PTSD, and others... well, some are practically catatonic. They just lay there, not responding to anyone and many barely eat when given food. Others haven't eaten since the monsters appeared. We do what we can for them, but while some people here have some kind of healing ability, no one has any ability to help with emotional trauma."

Shaking her head, Margret continued. "It's all so crazy. People have actual magic now. I saw someone who's arm had been nearly torn off, but just a couple hours later... it was like they'd never been injured. Well, here we are. Classroom fourteen is where you will be staying. The Ming family will be your roommates. This was the last room with only a single family in it. We are going to have to put three families to a room if we get any more survivors. We have a few dividers up. It's not much, but it's the best we can do for now. We are serving meals in the cafeteria. There will be a meeting in the gymnasium this afternoon that I think you should all attend. And one more thing, this is very important. I don't know if you've seen it happen, but we recommend that at least one person is awake at all times. Monsters sometimes appear out of nowhere, and if no one is keeping watching each of the rooms... well, we've lost some people when they were attacked in their sleep. We are working on a solution to this, and it will be discussed at the meeting."

Baron shared a grim look with Kassandra, while Rose hugged Drake to her side, and Kassie hugged her mom's leg. It didn't seem like the little girl understood everything, but she could read the mood and was clearly scared.

Margret left them to get to know their roommates and settle in.

The Ming family comprised Doctor Yang Ming, an old Chinese man who'd had an acupuncture business before the apocalypse. For being nearly eighty years old, he was remarkably spry. His eyes were clear and was in phenomenal health. He'd chosen the Path of Ki much like Baron had, but was farther along. He'd managed to clear three of his Meridians where Baron had only managed one so far. The old man had his granddaughter and two great grandchildren with him. Unfortunately, his granddaughter's husband hadn't survived.

Kassie recognized the youngest boy, Lee. He was one of her classmates and she immediately fell into playing with him.

Chapter 9

"Thank you for gathering for this meeting," Margret said. Almost all the people currently taking shelter in the small elementary school had gathered in the gymnasium.

Fortunately, since it was a school, there'd been plenty of folding chairs stored away to allow everyone a seat. "I would like to start us off by welcoming a fresh batch of survivors staying with us. Baron, Kassandra, Rose, Drake, and Kassie please, stand and be welcomed." Margret applauded vigorously, but only a half-hearted attempt at applause came back from the crowd. The family awkwardly stood there for a moment before resuming their seats.

"Thank you, everyone, for the warm welcome," Margret continued after silence filled the room again. "As most of you are aware, we'd formed a council of sorts to work together to understand everything that had been going on. We think we have come up with a few ideas and some actions we need to take that I will announce here today."

Margret shifted the papers on her podium until she found the one she needed. "I know we've been all concerned about the monsters appearing out of nowhere and attacking us in our sleep. One thing we, the council, discussed was a way to prevent it. In everyone's Status screen, there is a tab labeled Settlement. If you try to access it, it says that we currently only have two out of three necessary qualifications to access it. We have sufficient population and the school qualifies as an appropriate structure. But the System requires five thousand of these credits."

The principal took a sip from a glass of water before continuing. "You are all probably wondering why this tab is relevant. After consulting with those more familiar with these kinds of mechanics, as they call them, we're fairly certain that establishing a settlement will—at the very least—prevent these creatures from... spawning? I believe that is what they called it. We currently know of only one way to get these System Credits. Each of our scavenger teams, when they defeat one of these monsters, can... loot?

Margaret looked closer at her paper before continuing. "Yes, loot them and they usually receive meats, hides and other monster bits besides these System credits. if we have enough volunteers willing to go out and slay these things and return with this strange currency, we can accomplish two things at once. Not only will we be collecting the credits we need to turn this school into a recognized Settlement, but we will also make the immediate area around us safer. Fewer monsters should mean less monster attacks."

The crowd broke out into murmurs and one woman stood up and addressed the principal. "You want us to go out there and fight these demons? Are you insane? We'll all die!"

The crowd roared in response. The cacophony was chaotic, and it was hard to understand what anyone was actually saying. There was a lot of fear in the air and many people were close to panic at just the thought of going outside.

The principal tried to calm everyone down, but without a functioning microphone, she was just one more voice adding to the commotion. Doctor Ming stood up calmly. He adjusted his clothes to be as presentable as possible before taking a long, slow breath in. He held it for a moment and then opened his mouth. An earthy golden glow emanated from his mouth as his voice *boomed*, "Silence!"

The growing commotion was cut off in an instant. In the quiet that followed, Doctor Ming bowed slightly to the principal before retaking his seat.

"As I said, we are only looking for *volunteers* to go out and fight back against these monsters. I still don't understand why, or even how, but magic seems to be a real thing now. We have a man that is pouring water out of nowhere for us to drink. I've seen people healed in minutes from grievous injuries that should have needed an ER visit and months of recovery. Hell, Michael can conjure balls of fire in his bare hands. If we work together, go out in groups, and use these strange new abilities; we can make it. Now, with a show of hands, who will volunteer to fight to protect their friends and family?"

Margaret waited in silence for a moment while people considered and whispered amongst themselves. Baron looked over at Kassandra. She saw the look of determination in his eyes and knew what he wanted to do. She looked at her two children, then looked at Rose. "If we go out, will you take care of the kids... even if something happens to us?"

Rose thought about it for a minute. Drake was already her stepson and she would do her best to take care of him. Kassie had no relation to her, but whenever Kassie came over, Rose and John would treat her like one of their own. Before the apocalypse, John and her had joint custody of Drake. He'd spent every other week at their house, and half of the time his little sister stayed over on the weekends, too. Rose and Kassie had developed a strong bond already. There was no way she'd abandon the girl if something happened to her parents. "I will," Rose answered. "And you make sure you get back. Even if you're badly hurt, I'll heal you both and get you back on your feet. I've got Balder. He has already shown a willingness to protect us and you know he loves the kids. They'll be safe with me."

Baron nodded, then firmly raised his left hand. A second later, Kassandra's hand was raised as well. A few others had raised their hands to volunteer as well. Margaret stared for a moment at each person with their hand raised and noted down their name on a separate piece of paper.

"Ten volunteers are a good start. Would any of you that didn't volunteer to go hunting be willing to hold a watch on the roof? It should be safer than going out and will free up our current guard volunteers to go out as well."

A couple more minutes passed while the people talked quietly amongst themselves before a few more hands were raised. After noting them down, Margaret continued on with her address.

"Thank you for all the volunteers. Onto or next point of discussion, but still relevant to the previous. While Greg, the man responsible for us having drinking water, is working for over ten hours a day producing drinking water for everyone, he can't create enough by himself. Working himself to exhaustion each day, he can only produce about one hundred twenty gallons of water per day. There are now one hundred and seventy-six of us here. That means, until we have a better solution, we must ration our water. If our, for lack of a better term, hunter groups come across any bottled water, be it gallon jugs or bottles, if you can bring it back along with any food supplies you find, it will help us all immensely. Hopefully, this Settlement thing will have a solution to our water problem."

Margaret flipped to the next page in her notes and looked up with a smile. "Doctor Ming has volunteered to help anyone on the Path of Ki to understand and use their abilities. He'll stay behind once this meeting is over and organize a time that works with everyone."

Once the meeting came to a close, close to an hour later, lunch was served in the cafeteria. Rose took the children to get their food while Kassandra, Baron and the other volunteers met with the council to get organized. The line was long, but eventually they made their way to the front. Rose saw they had several propane camp stoves set up with huge stock pots that reminded her of John's forty-eight-quart pot he'd used to make his bone broth. Each person in line received a small bowl of soup. It had some vegetables and tiny chunks of meat floating in it. It didn't smell bad, but when they sat down and tried it, it was bland and not very filling.

Kassie only ate about half of her portion before refusing to eat any more, even after Rose tried to coax her into finishing. Drake, still hungry and not caring that it was bland, volunteered to finish it and drained it to the last drop. Rose's stomach still grumbled with hunger after she drank her bowl down, but after hearing about the rationing, she didn't complain or say anything about it. The kids needed the food more than she did.

57

Once they got back to their room, Rose gave Balder a portion of the dog food they'd brought along and he happily scarfed it down and lapped up some water. Kassie went to play with Lee again and Drake sat against the wall while petting his ball python. Rose had placed the leopard geckos in a tote that they had found and she looked at them in worry. They had decently fat tails, and could go awhile without eating, but she didn't know how she was going to feed them. Rose would normally go to the pet store each weekend to buy crickets for them, but that wouldn't be possible now. They also hadn't grown larger like Krom and Alma had. Krom and Alma might be able to hut for their own food if she let them outside, but Kitara, Toph and Luna wouldn't be able to handle the bigger insects she'd seen.

A while later, Baron, Kassandra and Doctor Ming came back into the room. They were talking amongst themselves when they entered and Baron pointed out Drake by the wall. With a nod, the old man walked over to Drake and sat down in front of the boy.

"Hello, your step-father and mother said you had chosen to be a Warrior and that you have a special sword," he said.

"Yeah," Drake answered, and glanced at his mom.

"I've learned a thing or two in my life about fighting. Would you like to learn some martial arts and how to use that Mana Blade of yours?"

"I suppose. What martial art?" Drake asked, showing some interest.

"I have been practicing Tai Chi and Wu-Shu since I was almost your age. I have already agreed to tutor your stepfather in meditation and Ki. Would you like to join us?"

"But I don't have Ki," Drake said.

"Meditation will help you focus and clear your mind. It will help anyone, not just those on the Path of Ki," Doctor Ming said.

"Ok, I'll try it. And then you'll teach me how to fight?"

The old man chuckled and answered, "I'll teach you how to better defend yourself."

After that, the old man stood up and invited Rose to join them in group meditation. Not seeing a problem with that, she agreed. Doctor Ming's granddaughter and her eleven-year-old daughter joined them. Rose had learned that the Granddaughter's name was Chunhua and her daughter's name was Huaban. They, like Doctor Ming, had chosen the Path of Ki.

Doctor Ming told everyone a bit about himself before he taught them how to meditate, including asking them to simply call him Yang, as it was his first name. He was a wonderful teacher, calm and able to get everyone to settle in and clear their minds. Over the first ten minutes, one by one, everyone gained the Meditation skill. It didn't work the same way for those on the Path of Mana as it did for Those on the Path of Ki. the Ki users gained better ability to visualize and control their Ki, helping them create it easier and form it into techniques, while the Mana users found that it actively increased their mana regeneration speed.

With the meditation practice, Rose felt calmer and more relaxed than she'd been in the last month. She could think clearly and not feel nearly as stressed, even with the apocalypse happening. She allowed herself to sink deeper into the meditation, letting time flow by and ignoring the soft *ping* she heard in her mind each time the skill advanced.

Chapter 10

Over the next several days, everyone fell into a routine. Drake, most of the children, and several adults, took part in regular training sessions with Dr. Ming. They'd start off the day with meditation to strengthen the mind, followed by various exercises in the gym to strengthen the body. Once the basic training was over, Dr. Ming would start martial arts training. The martial arts training was broken into two main parts: hand to hand and melee weapons.

Dr Ming had told them that, ordinarily, the students would go through years of hand to hand and stance work before transferring into weapon combat, but with the apocalypse... well, shortcuts had to be taken.

It was during the meditation training that Drake managed to learn a skill no one had heard of before. Drake had heard Dr. Ming talk to Baron about how to control and use Ki. The next morning, Drake tried to move his Mana around in the same way. he'd discovered that Mana didn't move in quite the same way, no predetermined pathways, and nothing to unblock or cleanse. It was when Drake managed to bring the mana to his fingertips—with a lot of effort—and cause a tiny blue spark to pop out of his skin that he'd gained the Mana Control skill.

Nobody knew what all could be done with Mana Control, but once Drake told Rose and his mom how he did it, they all buckled down to learn meditation and get that skill for themselves.

Several other discoveries were made during these few days. Magic beast cores had a use for people on the Path of Mana, two uses in fact. The cores could be absorbed by anyone who used Mana and they could either restore some of their Mana pool or gain some of the experience the creature contained. So, instead of leaving the little stones behind in favor of the meat and the leather, they were all gathered up. Those on the Path of Mana or who had someone on the Path in their family, would take them back and let them gain some experience points so they could level safely. Those on other Paths would naturally trade them to those who could use them.

Seeing how useful the Mana cores were, some cultivators tried to absorb the spirit and demon beast cores. Dr. Ming put a stop to that rather quickly. Since Dr. Ming had already opened his Brain Meridian, in addition to his Lung and Heart Meridians, he'd developed the ability to see the energies inside each person. The spirit and demon beast cores—especially the demon beast cores—tainted the Dantian, the Meridians they'd opened and even their Ki itself. Fortunately, the damage was minimal and Dr. Ming could use his acupuncture needles and his own Ki to help flush out the corruption and save their cultivation.

Baron and Kassandra worked as a team, and once they felt comfortable leaving Drake in the care of Dr. Ming, Rose joined them in hunting monsters and scavenging the nearby area. Before Rose joined them, Baron and Kassandra had to return after each fight to receive healing. Kassandra's stealth skills weren't yet up to allowing her to strike from the shadows, and she had no means of healing herself, unlike Baron, who learned pretty quickly how to use his Ki to recover from injuries. It wasn't as quick as magic spells or faith powers, but it was better than nothing. With Rose in the group to function as a healer and crowd control, and Balder acting as the group's tank, they all managed to take down more monsters safely. This led to considerably more loot being brought in. They saved all the cores from the monsters with levels to give to Drake, so he could level up while he underwent his training.

Baron had considered joining the martial arts training, but having completed combatives level two when he'd been in the army, he decided it was better to work at bringing in credits so they could have a safer place to live.

At the end of day four at the school, everyone who wasn't on watch had been gathered in the cafeteria for dinner. The community was only about five hundred credits away from being able to establish their official, System recognized Settlement, when a new prompt appeared in front of everyone at the same time.

Essence Stabilized
Analyzing...
Analyzing...
Average Essence Quality: Low
Native Sapient Survival Rate: 28.745333%
Initialization Stage One: Complete
Initialization Stage Two: Commencing

Congratulations, Native Sapients,
Your world "Earth" has achieved amazing survival rates
You are in the top 20% of newly initialized worlds for Survival Rate at the end of
Stage One

Stage Two Initialization
Imported entities increased in complexity
Dungeon spawning engaged
UI functionality improved
Stage Two Completion Requirement: Essence Quality Moderate

Before the System prompts appeared, the room was filled with a low buzz of conversation. People were enjoying the heartier meals they were getting, as there was a lot more meat to go around. Well, everyone except the vegetarians and the vegans. They had the hardest time getting enough to eat. Many of them eventually gave in and ate the same as everyone else. It was really only the most diehard vegans that were still trying to hold out, though they were getting a lot thinner than they were before the world ended.

Immediately after the system prompts appeared, the room fell dead silent. Once people had a moment to process the information, the silence turned into an uproar. Some people were clamoring for answers, others cried out at the death toll numbers, and overall, it was absolute chaos.

Margarete tried calming everyone down and bring the cafeteria back into order, but she was drowned out once again. Dr. Ming used his trick of magnifying his voice with Ki and got the silence the principal needed.

"I know this is confusing to some and very worrying to others, but we need to keep our heads. There is no need to panic. We can discuss this like adults," Margarete announced. "Let's first start off with this native sapient survival rate."

"What's sapient mean?" some guy in the crowd asked.

With a sigh, Margarete answered. "Sapient means something can think, has abstract thoughts and not just feelings or instincts. And I'm pretty sure it means us humans and that over five billion people have died in the last week."

The crowd got riled up again, but the former principal stepped in and nipped it in the bud. "As distressing as it is, there is nothing we can do about it right now. We have no means of communication, no method of transportation, no way to send or receive aid. We need to focus on the here and now. How we will survive and establish the System Settlement."

"What's that Dungeon thing?" someone else asked.

"I... I Don't—" Margarete said when someone else stood up and answered.

A young woman in her early twenties said, "It's a place where monsters spawn and you can go inside and kill them. You can get magic items and cool loot."

"I don't want to fight monsters," another woman said.

"I doubt you could run the first level anyway," the young woman replied. "Just hide away here while the rest of us gain levels. More loot for me."

"I can make the Settlement," another man called out. "There is a City Core on the perk list."

"Hold on. Just give me a minute, and no one choose a perk just yet. We need to be smart about this. Give me a moment to pull it up," Margarete said while holding her hands up in a stop gesture. She then poked her finger a couple times in the air and stared off into the middle distance as she read the options quickly.

As she was about to open her mouth to speak, the ground shuddered. Closing her mouth and looking around, like almost everyone else, Margarete tried to figure what was going on.

"Woah," someone called out in alarm. When Margarete looked at who shouted, she saw someone's head rise about a foot higher than everyone else before he fell straight down and out of sight. People started screaming and several more people that had been standing next to the man fell out of sight. Everyone started pushing into each other, trying to get away.

Baron leaped to his feet, along with Kassandra and Rose. As the crowd pulled away from the center of the commotion, they could see what seemed like a sinkhole. A couple seconds later, a pair of segmented black sticks poked out of the hole and waved around, shortly followed by a round chitinous head with large compound eyes and even larger

63

pincers. The rest of the ant-like creature crawled out on its six legs. It looked just like an ant, except it was the size of a football.

Baron strode forward to stomp the enormous insect, until he saw several more pairs of antennae poking out of the hole, followed quickly by even more. Within a handful of seconds, over a dozen ants were crawling out, and more were following.

The ants formed groups of nearly half a dozen each and charged at the humans closest to the hole. They swarmed each person, grabbing the people with their powerful pincers, knocking them down and dragging them into the hole.

One of the fire mages started throwing fire bolts into the hole, and that started a whole barrage of ranged attack spells being thrown. Not everyone had the best aim, though. Many of the shots completely missed their mark and landed amongst the crowd, increasing the screams and general chaos.

A series of hissing screeches and loud clacking came from the hole. A veritable horde of ants came storming out. Some were singed or missing chunks of exoskeleton, but the vast majority were still whole.

Baron had to duck one of those errant blasts, turned quickly and picked up Kassie with his good arm while yelling, "We need to get out of here!" Fortunately, they were fairly close to the doors leading out of the cafeteria. Baron used the enhanced strength he gained from opening his Muscle Meridian and forced a path through the panicked people, Kassandra, Rose, and Drake, practically on his heels.

They ran to their room first to grab what they could and collect the animals, they'd left the dogs in their room with some fresh meat to eat. Rose collected the reptiles quickly, a task made easier with her animal communication spell.

As they left the room they'd been living in for the last four days, they spotted a pack of ants following their trail. Krom and Alma darted forward and snapped up an ant each, crushing them in their jaws and swallowing them down. Uni, Kassandra's Soul-Bound Pomsky, happily chomped on one, crushing it in her jaws, until the ant's juices squirted in her mouth, then she couldn't drop it fast enough.

Baron stomped on one with his large boot. It died almost instantly, but another of the ants bit through the leather and the only thing that kept Baron's toes attached was the steel cap under the leather. "Damn it!" Baron roared as he punted the ant into the wall.

It bounced off and scurried back to him. Kassandra stabbed it with one of her knives as Drake cut another one in half with his Mana blade.

Balder managed to kill the last one, but he reacted like Uni had, doing his best to rid his tongue of the nasty taste it left in his mouth.

As they ran down the hall, towards the front door, Kassandra spoke up. "Where are we going to go? What are we going to do?"

"I don't know, but it's not safe here. There are too many of those giant ants, and there is no way we can stop them. This is their home now."

As they made the last turn to the door, Rose looked back down the hall that lead to the cafeteria. People were still scrambling to get out of the room, tripping over and trampling on anyone who was in their way. They were followed by hundreds of ants that were pouring out of the doors and into the hallway. Baron burst through the doorway and they all ran out into the falling night.

Chapter 11

Dozens of people had already made it outside before Rose and her group, and more pushed their way through the door behind them. They'd all scattered in every direction, a choice made in panic that many paid for with their lives. Ambush predators, ones that usually hid from the hunting parties, came out in force. Rose could only assume that the screaming and the increased scent of blood in the air had alerted the monsters to a potential feast.

Only a few smaller groups managed to fight off the attacks. Those groups had members who leveled and increased their skills by hunting these beasts. The rest, well... they hid away where they had thought that they were safe, hoping the world would go back to the way it was.

"Where are we going to go?" Kassandra asked. Her voice was tight with the sudden stress from the attack.

"Away from here," Baron grunted his answer as he slashed his Soul-Bound blade through a monstrous feline's neck. He deftly stepped away from the gout of blood that sprayed from the decapitated corpse. He looked around quickly, spotting a more or less quiet area that seemed to be devoid of people or monsters he pointed. "That way, for now."

As the group ran, Baron, Kassandra and her familiar ranged ahead of the group, clearing any of the monsters that appeared in their path. Rose and Balder stayed with the children, with Kassie doing her best to keep up with everyone. She had the lowest stats of the group, her highest attributes being only eight points. No one bothered trying to loot the monsters they slayed, only focusing on getting away and finding somewhere relatively safe to spend the night.

It took nearly half an hour before they felt like they had gotten far enough away from the chaotic slaughter. They'd made their way into a small post office branch. The glass front doors had already been smashed. Kassandra used her Fade ability to sneak in to check it out. The building had been fully ransacked, not a single intact package survived. It was clear of any squatters and there were no signs of monsters in the building, so they settled on sleeping in one of the back rooms.

"I'm hungry," Kassie whined. Her feet dragged as they made their way inside, as though her shoes were made of lead.

"I know, baby girl," Kassandra said. "Do we have anything to eat or drink?"

Rose looked around, only just realizing that none of them had a bag of any kind. They'd only just sat down to eat dinner when the System prompt appeared in front of everyone. When they got to their room, she had been so focused on getting her animals that she had forgotten to grab some supplies. Guilt made her feel like she had a heavy weight in her stomach. *Why didn't I grab something, anything? Even some granola bars would have been better than nothing.* "Um... I didn't grab any supplies, did any of you?"

Baron shook his head. Drake looked down at his feet and mumbled a quiet, "No."

Kassandra stroked Kassie's hair softly. "I'm sorry, we don't have anything."

Kassie curled into her mom and wept softly.

Baron looked at everyone in the group. They were all dirty, sweaty, and tired looking. It had been a sudden and stressful evening right after things had just settled down. "Stay here. I'm going to see what I can find nearby."

"You can't. It's already dark out," Kassandra said.

"It's too dangerous," Rose said.

"We need food and drink. There is nothing here and none of us brought anything with us. I'll be fine. I won't go far."

"We will be fine with missing one meal," Kassandra said firmly. "It's better to wait until morning. We don't know what's out there. What's stopping something from jumping you out of the shadows?"

"The kids have already had a terrifying day. I will not make them go to sleep hungry on top of that, if I can help it. We fucked up and didn't grab any supplies. That's on us... It's on me. *I'll* make it right. Besides, I saw a laundromat that probably has a vending machine or two and a couple shops only a block away. I won't be gone long."

"You can't go alone," Kassandra said as she gently pried Kassie off and passed her to Rose. "If you must go out," Kasandra sighed, "I'll go with you. Uni can stay here to help

67

protect the kids with Rose and Balder." They all knew how stubborn Baron could get. Sometimes, it was better to work with him than to obstruct him.

Baron looked like he was about to argue, but when he met the the steely look in Kassandra's eye, his shoulders slumped and he just sighed, "Fine."

Rose settled in, leaning her back against the wall. Kassie snuggled into her lap. Uni whined at the door Kassandra and Baron had just left through. "It's okay Uni, come here girl," Rose said while patting the floor next to her. The small dog trotted over and curled up next to Rose, eyes fixed on the door. After a few minutes of getting petted, she calmed down and half closed her eyes as she enjoyed the attention.

"What's going to happen to us?" Drake asked out of nowhere.

Rose looked at Drake. The boy looked more like his father every day, and right now he seemed to carry the weight of the world on his shoulders. He was sitting across the small room from her, fiddling with the hilt of his Mana Blade, staring into the middle distance.

"I, I don't know, sweetie. Nothing like this has ever happened before," Rose answered.

"Are we going to die?"

Tears were forming in the corners of his eyes, and his lips trembled. Rose's heart ached when she heard his question. She didn't know how to answer him. So many people had died already, billions of lives lost. It was amazing that they'd survived as long as they had, but she couldn't say that. She also couldn't honestly say that they wouldn't die, either. Rose realized that she had taken too long to come up with the right answer a moment later.

"I don't want to die," Drake sobbed out.

*　　　　　　*　　　　　　*

"Okay, why did you really want to come out here?" Kassandra asked after they had left the small post office.

Baron looked at her for a moment before answering. "I felt something strange when we arrived. It was at the very edge of my Spiritual Sense."

"What was it?"

"I don't know. It kept flickering in and out of my perception," Baron answered.

"Why didn't you just say so? Or that you wanted to scout around the building before we settled in for the night?"

"First, I did plan on trying to find some food and water while I was out. Second, well… I didn't want to worry the kids any more than they already were."

"Fine," Kassandra said with exasperation. "It was still a dumb plan to come out here by yourself. You only have the one defensive technique figured out so far, so all you can do is stab things. At least I can teleport and shoot things with my magic. So where was this thing you were sensing? Is it still there?"

Baron closed his eyes for a moment as he tried to detect the flickering presence. Kassandra was jealous of the ability. No one she knew, besides those on the Path of Ki, had any extra sensory perceptions. Even after learning the basics of Mana control, she could only feel her own Mana, not someone else's.

"I feel it. It's less like flickering and more like something is… pulsating?. It's not Ki based though, maybe Mana? It's hard to get a good read," Baron said. His eyes were still closed and his head was cocked to the side, like he was listening intently for something. After another moment, he turned towards an alley next to the post office. Baron opened his eyes and pointed down the alley with his blade. "It's down there."

Kassandra conjured a globe of darkness in her left hand while pulling out a knife with her right. "Well, let's check it out," she said just before activating her Fade ability and entered stealth. Even though She had only reached the second rank of Mana Control, she had already gained one benefit from the skill. Before, she wasn't able to hold her Dark Bolt spell for more than a couple of seconds. Now, with better control over her Mana, she could hold it for a couple minutes before it lost cohesion and detonated in her hand.

I wish I had a dark vision spell. Kassandra thought as she crept through the shadows. Her night vision skill helped a bit, and had even ranked up just before they made it to the post office. *It's ridiculous that a rogue with dark magic doesn't have some kind of dark sight ability.* She shook her head to clear her errant thoughts and forced her mind to focus on what she was doing.

69

Up ahead, maybe fifty-feet away, Kassandra thought she could just make out something with a faint pulsing blue glow. She looked over her shoulder and saw that Baron was only about twenty feet behind her. With Fade active, Baron couldn't detect her, but they'd worked out a steady pace for him to use while she was stealthed, so he wouldn't overtake her.

After waiting for a couple moments for Baron to get closer, and not seeing or hearing anything else in the alley with them, Kassandra broke her stealth and dropped Fade. "I think I see it, right over there. Something has a faint blue glow. Can you make it out?" she whispered.

Baron peered into the darkness. He regretted not opening his Brain Meridian sooner, like Dr. Ming had recommended. The Muscle, Dermal and Bone Meridians were great for combat, but for things like seeing in the dark, or actually being able to see energies, they were useless. His wife had higher ranks in the perception skills, so could see and hear better than he could, but between her help pointing it out and his Spiritual Sense, he'd found what she was talking about. "Yeah, I think I see it. What is it?" he whispered back.

"Do you feel anything else nearby?"

"No, I don't. I'm a little concerned about that, to be honest. It feels like we are walking into a trap."

Kassandra sheathed her knife and pulled a pebble out of her pocket. "Let's see if we can spring it," she said while bouncing the thumbnail sized rock in her palm.

Baron nodded to her and readied himself for whatever may spring out.

Kassandra threw the pebble and the *clack, clack, clack* it made as it skittered and bounced sounded louder in their ears than any pebble had the right to. They waited there, muscles tense and spell ready to fly. Seconds passed, and they continued to wait... and after what felt like an eternity, with nothing springing out, they relaxed a bit and slowly approached.

Kassandra and Baron gave each other confused glances when they got close enough to see what the hell it was. A small blue crystalline orb lay in the trash. It was transparent and pulsed with the regular rhythm of a heartbeat. Kassandra stared at it until it triggered her Identify skill.

70

"Were you able to identify it?" Baron asked. "I got nothing but question marks."

"Um... yeah... it's something called a Spell Orb. It says it can grant a random spell to whomever holds it." Kassandra answered. Her brow was scrunched up in confusion as she tried to understand. "Where did it come from? Have you seen anything like it?"

"I don't know. I mean, once in a great while, one of the hunters might get some weird piece of loot from a monster kill. I mean, aside from the usual monster parts. One guy got a carved bone neckless that increased his dexterity by a point. But no, nothing like this. Do you think it's safe?"

"It should be. No one has been lied to by one of these prompts before that I know of," Kassandra answered. She felt the Dark Bolt in her hand quiver, and it was growing more difficult to control the Mana the longer she held it, so she pointed up at the sky and let it go. After it flew over a hundred feet, it broke apart and dispersed back into Essence. With her hand now free, she reached out and picked up the Orb.

The moment her skin touched the crystal-like sphere, it stopped pulsing with blue light and turned completely black. By the time she stood back up with it gripped in her hand, it had shifted to a black so dark that it seemed like she was holding a hole in the universe. As she looked at the strange object, she felt a popping sensation from it. Like a sheet of glass, faster than the eye could track, cracks spread across the ball and it shattered into thousands of pieces that dissolved as fast as they fell.

Congratulations,
You have gained the spell Dark Vision from a Spell Orb.

Chapter 12

After being gone for close to two hours, Baron and Kassandra returned to the post office with a couple of bags filled with chocolate bars, mini bags of chips, and bottles of soda.

"I was getting worried there for a bit. You guys have been gone so long," Rose said with a sigh of relief.

"Sorry about that. We had to wait out a patch of trouble. Some idiots were fighting over a few rolls of toilet paper. And by fight, I mean throwing balls of fire, blades of air and trying their best to kill each other," Kassandra said. "I think the rolls of toilet paper were burned up in the mess. They probably would have managed to actually kill each other, but Slenderman got to them first." Kassandra shuddered at the recent memory.

"Wait, Slenderman? That urban myth kids made up?" Rose asked.

"Yeah, that's what Identify called it. It was creepy as hell. It was nearly eight feet tall, with elongated arms and legs and no face. It snuck up on the brawlers, and… and it… it fucking ripped them apart. We hid until it was long gone."

Rose shuddered at the mental image. "Well, at least you guys are safe. The kids are worried and hungry." Rose glanced at the bags of food pointedly.

"Right," Kassandra said. shaking her head, she started pulling items out and passing them around. Nutrition wise, they didn't make the best dinner, but it was better than nothing.

The room fell quiet aside from the rustle of wrappers and the crunch of over-processed starchy food. Once the food was finished, and everyone was satisfied enough to get by, Baron brought up a topic of discussion.

"I think we should decide what to do with our Moderate Perks. I think we are going to need every advantage we can get right now, especially without the shelter of the school and people in it for support. Have any of you looked over the options yet?"

"I actually did while we were waiting for you to get back," Rose said.

"What are your thoughts?" Baron asked.

"Well, one of the options was for that Settlement Core thing mentioned at the meeting. Maybe one of us should get that? It might make this post office into a safe place."

"If there were more of us, then... maybe. But after seeing people try to kill each other for fucking toilet paper, it might just paint a huge target on our backs as everyone tries to take it for themselves," Baron said while shaking his head.

"What about the vehicle option?" Kassandra asked as she scrolled through the options.

Baron shook his head. "Again, I think it would place a target on us. We don't have enough strength to fight off the monsters and the people at the same time. And where would we go? Nowhere is safe anymore. I think we should choose something that will increase our immediate capabilities, something that will increase our chances of surviving but won't make us more visible to others."

"What about Kassie?" Kassandra asked. "I have a prompt to choose her perk as well. It has more options than the first one did."

"What are the options?" Baron asked.

Since Kassie wasn't her daughter, Rose stayed out of their discussion and contemplated her own options. The Archetype Tome sounded interesting, but she wasn't sure skills alone would be the best option, and she didn't even know which archetype to choose. Resetting her Path with the Reset Crystal didn't appeal to her either. She was happy enough with her original choice.

The portable workshop, Vehicle and settlement Core were out, and she just couldn't see herself walking around with Power Armor, it was the opposite of low profile.

"Okay, the Soul-Bound Beast Companion it is then," Rose heard Baron say. She looked up from her list and paid attention to their discussion.

"Kassie, what kind of pet would you like?" Kassandra asked.

The little girl cocked her head to the side in thought. Then she held up the children's picture book she had been looking at. Her face lit up and pointed at one animal on the page. "That! I want Mr. Fox."

Baron and Kassandra looked at each other in silent communication. She shrugged, and he lifted one shoulder. Kassandra turned back to her daughter. "Are you sure you want a fox pet?"

"Yes! I want Mr. Fox. I can pet him, hold him, and he is super smart."

"I can't guarantee it will be a boy fox, are you okay with that?" Kassandra asked.

She got an enthusiastic nod in return, so waiting no longer, she pressed her finger on the option. A few seconds later, a spot on the floor in front of Kassie glowed white. The light formed an egg-like shape as it grew brighter. With a near blinding flash, an egg the size of a football appeared, and the light vanished.

The egg rocked several times before enormous cracks formed on the shell. A moment later, the egg shattered into tiny pieces that dissolved seconds after hitting the floor. In its place lay a golden-red fox kit, curled up with its fluffy tail draped over its nose.

Rose used Identify on the creature.

| Nine-Tailed Kitsune Kit |
| Body Rank 0 |

Rose knew she needed to work on her Identify skill, it was still very low level and didn't provide much information. It was hard to remember to use it enough to level it.

"What are you going to name it?" Rose asked.

Kassandra thought for a long moment before asking, "Is it a boy or girl?"

Baron gently picked up the sleeping animal and looked under its single tail. "It's a girl," he said. "and isn't it supposed to be a nine-tailed fox? Why does it only have one tail?"

"She is Foxie," Kassie declared with all the confidence of a seven-year-old. She then ran up and scooped the baby fox out of Baron's hand and hugged it close. The poor kit woke up startled, wriggled out of Kassie's grip and ran to a corner of the room.

Tears formed in the corner of Kassie's eyes, and her lips trembled. Seeing the potential for a full-blown meltdown, Kassandra moved quickly to cut it off. "It's okay, Kassie. She was just scared. She is a baby and just woke up. Here, offer her this and see if she will come to you." Kassandra handed her daughter a piece of jerky left over from their makeshift dinner.

"Now, move slowly and quietly," Kassandra instructed.

Kassie did as her mother instructed and slowly approached the baby fox with the food outstretched. When she was only a few feet away, her mother had her stop and sit down on the floor. After a couple of long minutes, the shaking fox's nose twitched at the smell and poked her head out from under her tail.

It took a couple more minutes before Foxie built up enough courage to slowly creep closer to Kassie. Rose's heart melted as the two got to know each other. It didn't take too much longer before the little fox was licking the girl's face, driving her into helpless giggles.

Rose turned to Drake. "So, what do you want to pick?"

"Umm... I was thinking... maybe Bloodline," Drake mumbled.

"Bloodline? That wasn't an option for me. What is it?"

"It's like in Naruto... You know how the Uchiha have the Sharingan, well that's their bloodline ability. I think it's something like that."

"You know it won't be the same, right?" Rose asked.

"Yeah, I know. But I'm sure it will still be some kind of cool, awesome ability. I bet I'll become super strong in no time."

"I don't see why not, but let's check with your mom fir... s... t," Rose was saying before she noticed Drake already stabbing his finger into thin air. He hadn't waited to hear the rest of what she was saying. The moment she said she didn't see why not; he took that as permission and picked his perk.

Mere moments after making his selection, swirls of tiny black flames consumed his eyes, turning them into pitch black, rotating orbs. Red light emitted from their depths, casting a radiant aura similar to the edge of his Mana Blade.

After Drake's eyes finished their transformation, red edged black wisps rose from his back, starting with just a few, but the volume rapidly increased until it looked like a bonfire raged out of his back. With a great *whoosh,* the black flames spread out to either side and took on the form of huge bird wings.

75

"What the actual *fuck*! What did you do?" Kassandra yelled.

Rose turned and saw Baron and Kassandra rushing over, fear clearly etched into their faces.

"I got the Shadow Phoenix bloodline. It's sooo cool," Drake said. The boy had a huge grin on his face, which honestly looked rather intimidating with the black and red eyes and burning wings.

"You did *what?* Drake, what… how… I… you… you're *literally* on fire!" Baron stammered out.

It took quite a while for everyone to calm down. It wasn't until Drake managed to turn off the burning wings and terrifying black eye effects that Baron and Kassandra calmed enough to have a reasonable discussion. They weren't happy that Drake had chosen his perk without consulting them, especially without warning them before the dramatic revelation. However, once he shared the prompt that explained the abilities he got from the bloodline, they had to admit that it was a good choice.

Congratulations!
You have unlocked a Bloodline ability
Bloodline: Shadow Phoenix's Flame

Bloodline Ability: Shadow Phoenix Fire
Congratulations, one of your distant ancestors was an evolved Legendary Beast, the Phoenix. The intense fire of your ancestor merged with your Dark flame Soul Element to create the powerful and restorative ability known as the Shadow Phoenix Fire.

Shadow Flame Wings: Manifest the wings of your ancestor, these wings provide enhanced mobility and high defense. Uses: 3/day, Duration: 1 minute x Constitution Score

Shadow Flame Shield: Use your wings to block or deflect attacks.
Defense: 2 x Level

Healing Fire: Consume the fire from your wings to recover Health.
Heal: 3 x Level + Constitution score
Note: Consume Shadow Flame Wings on use.

Detonation: Overload your Shadow Flame Wings with Mana to create a 10-foot radius explosion centered on yourself.
Damage = (2 x lvl) + 1 for every 2 Mana spent.
Note: Consumes Shadow Flame Wings on use, you are Immune to Detonation

Baron ended up choosing to enhance his existing Soul-Bound weapon, which gave it some interesting properties. Before, Baron could use Ki to heat the blade, causing burning damage and increase its size. The enhanced version did the same, but it also could change more than its size. After it finished its upgrade, Baron shared its new stats.

Solblade Gauntlet
Quality: Exceptional
Rarity: Rare
Durability: 80/80
Damage: 12 dagger form, 34 burning sword form
Weight: 1.5 lbs.
Traits: crit chance +10% dagger form
Ki effects: Ki pool regenerates at 1 point per 10 minutes. Infuse Ki into blade to deal fire damage (1:2) infuse 10 points of Ki to extend blade to 3 feet for 5 minutes. Deals an extra 10 fire damage.
Enhanced Ki effects: grafted to arm, functions as prosthetic hand with full sensory input.
Forms: Gauntlet: defense 20, Fully functional Prosthetic.
Blade: 12-inch Dagger. Infuse with Ki to deal fire damage, infuse with 10 Ki to extend blade to 3 feet dealing +10 fire damage.
Ki blaster: Condenses fire Ki into a gelatinous sphere that launches at a high rate of speed. Sphere bursts on impact, clinging to the target. Assisted targeting through Interface. Range: 50ft per body rank. Damage: 20 Ki per shot- 60 fire damage + 5dmg/second for 12 seconds.
Ki pool: 100/100

After sharing the stats on his Soul-Bound weapon, Baron stopped paying attention to anything else for the next hour. He spent that entire time marveling at his new prosthetic hand. He would flex his metallic fingers over and over, run his fingers over every surface, amazed at the sensation he felt.

While Baron was focused on his new hand, Kassandra decided she wanted a weapon that would pack a punch. She chose the enhanced soul-bound Weapon for herself. It was then that they discovered that, unlike with the Minor Perk, you didn't need to use a weapon on hand. The Medium Perk would let you choose a weapon type and it would appear before you like the Kassie's fox did.

Kassandra chose a sword, similar to a Katana but with a straight edge, a bit shorter, and a more angular point.

Shadow Striker
Soul-Bound, Dark Steel Ninjato
Quality: Exceptional
Rarity: Rare
Durability: 60/60
Damage: 24
Weight: 3lbs
Material Bonus: Dark Steel - Weakness: When damage is dealt target suffers -1 Str/3 ranks of dark magic for 30 seconds

Shadow's Edge: Bypass 30% defense. Cost: 30 Mana

Tainted Blade: Deal poison damage equal to attack's damage over 30 seconds. Mana Cost: 40.

Shadow Strike: x2 damage after using shadow step.
Mana Pool: 200

That just left Rose to choose her Medium Perk. Between the six reptiles and her dog Balder, she felt she had enough animals to manage, so the Rare beast companion was off the table for her. Since she didn't have the option to choose a Bloodline ability, and after seeing how powerful each of the enhanced Soul-Bound weapons were, she decided she might as well get one for herself. Rose just hoped that she could get one that wasn't so... up close and personal.

After selecting that option, she scrolled down the huge list of available weapons she could choose from. All the classic medieval style weapons were there, and even some gun-like weapons. While she had some practice at the shooting range with her husband, she didn't feel comfortable enough to rely on one in a life-or-death struggle. It wasn't until she got to a selection of Mage Staffs, that Rose felt that she had found one that suited her. She made her choice, and it appeared.

Staff of Nature's Might
Soul-Bound Wyrdwood Mage Staff

Quality: Exceptional
Rarity: Rare
Durability: 50/50
Damage: 12
Weight: 3lbs
Material Bonus: Wyrdwood - Mana conductive: spells channeled through this staff receive -10% Mana cost. x2 Item Mana Pool
Magic effects:
Nature's Might: Plant magic spell effect increased by 2% per level

Wall of thorns: Grow a living thorn filled hedge. Dimensions: 10ft tall x 30ft long x 5ft thick. Duration: until Hedge dies. Mana Cost: 40.

Bark skin: skin takes on the texture and hardness of Ironbark but retains normal flexibility. Defense: +30, Duration: 10 min, Mana Cost: 50.

Nature's domain: Cleanse disease, poison, regenerate 1hp per minute, +30% mana and stamina regen for all in its area. AOE: 20 ft, Duration: 1hr, Mana cost: 400.
Mana Pool: 400

Rose was very satisfied with her new staff. In her personal opinion, it provided everything they would need to survive the crazy and dangerous world they found themselves in. *Now, if only I knew where John was. Would he even recognize me? I'm thinner than I have ever been in my entire life. Everything is so different now; would he even love me still?* Rose shook her head, trying to rid herself of her intrusive thoughts. Even now, after the System took away her ADHD and Bi-Polar disorder, she still had to deal with the ingrained behavior patterns. Remembering what John would say when she had intrusive thoughts, Rose breathed in deeply and began her grounding exercises.

Chapter 13

"GET DRAKE AND KASSIE INSIDE," Baron bellowed as his mechanical hand morphed into a three-foot-long sword. He blocked the scythe-like forelimb of a giant praying mantis before he swept his whole arm back and severed the limb at the shoulder.

Rose regretted having to leave the small post office that morning, but a pack of mutated feral cats managed to sneak their way inside just before dawn. They 'd managed to fight off the beasts, suffering a few injuries in the process. But the blood and viscera left behind after looting the corpses would have drawn scavengers like a magnet. *Poor leopard geckos. They tried to help fight off the cats, but they were too weak to survive.*

Rose shook her head to clear the distracting thoughts as she dragged Drake into the convenience store. His little sister followed closely behind. Kassie clutched at the small fox in her arms, trying to hold back the tears and the screams that wanted to crawl out of her throat.

As soon as Drake was inside and away from the giant insects, Rose pulled the severed mantis blade from his stomach. He groaned in pain as blood welled out of the ghastly wound. Rose moved her staff over Drake's body while she spent five seconds casting her Plant Magic spell, Nature's Boon. The green gem at its head glowed with a soft emerald light. The spell wasn't very powerful, but it would stabilize Drake and restore twenty-five Health over the next five minutes.

"Balder, protect Drake and Kassie," Rose ordered.

Balder stood between the kids and the front of the store; his fur shifted to a slate gray and his fangs took on a translucent crystalline appearance. He was ready.

Kassandra rose from the mantis' shadow. Her Soul-Bound sword gathered black shadows along its blade like a sticky tar as it slashed towards the back of the monster. The blade cut easily through the carapace, causing a deep, bleeding wound. The shadow stuff clung to the wound, seeping in to the creature's blood and causing two debuffs. The mantis' blows against Baron grew weaker, its Strength dropped by five points, and its Health fell steadily from the poison-like effect.

Baron's sword glowed a deep cherry red as he infused his Ki into his Soul-Bound weapon. He thrust it deep into the mantis while it was distracted by the attack from behind. The blade pierced its armor, and he dragged the blade up through its thorax and out near its neck. The stench of the bug's burning innards invaded everyone's nostrils and made them want to gag.

The mantis toppled over from the various injuries it suffered, dead. Kassandra looted the monster while Rose lifted her Staff of Nature's Might, the gem glowing brighter as she activated one of the staff's abilities. A series of vines broke through the concrete covering the ground and interwove themselves into a thick wall of vegetation. Thorns, as long as her fingers and sharp enough to score steel, grew everywhere. Anything that tried to make its way through that would pay the price in blood and flesh.

Kassandra knelt by her son, and checked on his condition. The bleeding had slowed, and the wound was closing.

Baron's sword shifted back to his gauntlet-looking, prosthetic hand before he collapsed inside the convenience store. With exhaustion filling his voice, he said, "Good choice for your Medium Perk, Rose. How long will that thorny hedge stay up?"

"It doesn't have a timer on it, So I think it will stay as long as it survives. It's an actual plant instead of something conjured." Rose was still trying to get a handle on her new staff and its abilities.

Kassie curled up in her father's lap, seeking comfort and protection from the chaotic world.

Drake slowly sat up—his arm shifting to his midsection when the movement caused him to wince in pain. "Take it easy. You took a hard hit," Kassandra said. The worry for her son was clear in her voice.

"I wish Dad was here," Drake said quietly, while tears leaked from the corner of his eyes.

"I know, dear. I'm sure he is okay. Knowing John, he's probably already halfway home by now," she said. None of them, not even John's wife Rose, knew where he was or even if he was still alive, but they had to do their best to keep hope alive.

Everyone started for a moment as two large mounds rose from the turned earth at the base of the thorn wall. Then, the group breathed a collective sigh of relief when the reddish head of Krom and the tan head of Alma broke through the soil. The beardies weren't as fast over long distances as the rest of the group, so it always took them a bit of time to catch up. They clambered out of the tunnel they created; their two-foot-long bodies and even longer tails took a few seconds to clear the holes. It didn't help that it looked like they had gorged on one of the dead insects that they hadn't managed to loot.

Apophis followed closely behind. It had only been about three and a half feet long before the apocalypse, but now it was the size of a reticulated python and could cultivate its own Ki.

*   *   *

Rose let out a deep sigh. The wounds Baron and Drake suffered at the giant mantises' claws were recovering well, and they all seemed safe for now.

Rose was suddenly torn away from her musings as a familiar *crack* echoed from outside, followed by several more. Rose hadn't heard that sound since John had taken her to the gun range on his last home time.

Everyone in the convenience store froze at the sound of gunfire. Baron looked at Kassandra, confusion written across his face as he flexed his gauntlet-like prosthetic hand.

Rose watched as Baron slowly stood up and quietly approached the thicket she'd grown. They could hear the faint sounds of people yelling and insect screeching. *How do people have guns? How are they able to use them without them exploding in their hands?* Rose wondered.

After a few minutes of gunshots and yelling, everything grew quiet outside. "It's safe to come out now. The monsters are dead." A man called out in the silence.

After a moment of not hearing a reply, he called out again. "My name is Corporal Higgins; my men and I are from the army base and we are gathering survivors together. We have a safe place where we can protect civilians. Come on out, you won't be harmed."

Baron, Kassandra, and Rose gathered together and conversed in a whisper.

"Can we trust them?" Kassandra asked.

"I don't know," Baron answered. "We've all seen how people have turned into little more than beasts, killing over a fucking roll of toilet paper."

"But what if it's true? What if they have a safe place? Drake almost died; Kassie can't even defend herself," Rose said.

Kassandra looked over at her kids in worry. There *had* been too many close calls. She turned back to Baron, "Should we try? If they are with the army, they should have food too, right?"

Baron's stomach rumbled at the thought of food. The convenience store they sheltered in had already been picked clean, and they were all on short rations.

"We know you're in the convenience store, behind the hedge. Just come on out. We're not going to hurt you," the Higgins said. There was an edge of irritation in his voice that hadn't been there before. He seemed to be losing patience.

"I don't know," Baron whispered. "I have a bad feeling about this."

"But what are we going to do?" Rose asked. "They know we're in here. We don't have anywhere to go."

"Maybe I should go scout it out," Kassandra said.

As they pondered their options, they heard another, much quieter voice speak. "Why don't we just go in and drag them out? You know *Lord* Jackson is getting impatient. We're only a few people short of becoming a small town. He doesn't care how we get them in, just that we get them."

"Shit," Baron swore. "We need to get out of here."

"How are your Ki levels?" Kassandra asked. "My Mana's full. What about you Rose?"

"I've only got half of my Ki pool, but it'll have to do," Baron answered.

"My Mana is full too," Rose said as she gripped her Soul-Bound staff tightly. Rose reached out through her beast magic and readied all of her pets. Balder stood up and moved next to her stepson, Drake. Alma and Krom, shifted back to the small tunnel they had dug to get inside and stood just outside of the hole. Apophis just laid there; the nearly ten-foot-long ball python merely twitched her head toward the thick bramble-like wall and flicked her tongue.

Kassandra got up and moved over to where the two kids were sleeping. Covering their mouths so they wouldn't make any noise, she whispered, "You need to wake up. We're going to need to run again."

Drake jerked awake and recoiled from his mother's grip. It took him a moment to come to his senses, then he nodded. Kassie, who was snuggled in with her Soul-Bound fox only squirmed and tried to snuggle in deeper with her warm pet.

Kassandra released Drake as he got up. She then turned her attention to her daughter and gently shook her until Kassie finally opened her eyes. Kassie still looked exhausted. While her mother used Kassie's minor perk to double the little girl's Stamina pool, it didn't help with her Regen rate. Kassie groaned but sat up at her mother's bidding.

Baron stood next to the hedge, his prosthetic hand already transfigured into a Metroid-looking blaster cannon, one of the four forms it could take.

In the silence, just a minute after the second man spoke, the leader spoke again, but quietly, as if to his companion. "Fuck it. I'm tired of this shit. Peterson, burn me a way in."

Everyone heard a loud *whoosh*, and the wall of vines smoked.

With the sudden speed reptiles were known for, the two-foot-long bearded dragons and the snake darted through the hole.

There was a *snap-hiss* as Drake activated his Soul-Bound Mana-blade. He approached the smoking plant wall to stand alongside Baron and Rose.

Rose shook her head and said, "No, stay back and protect your sister."

"Balder is protecting her. I can fight." Drake said back.

"Do as she said. Protect your sister." Baron said in a tone that brooked no nonsense.

84

Sullenly, Drake moved to the back of the main room, where Kassie stood holding Foxie. Balder's fur had already taken on the slate-gray coloration that showed his armor ability was activated, and his fangs had enlarged and turned crystalline.

"Where's mommy?" Kassie asked.

Drake looked around and only just then noticed his mother had disappeared. Her disappearance wasn't a surprise to him. Kassandra was a Rogue on the Path of Mana and had access to the shadow school of magic. She would disappear, only to reappear from a monster's shadow and deal devastating damage to it.

Once the fire had managed to burn through most of the hedge, there was a scream of pain from outside, followed by the clatter of bullets being fired. As though that was his signal, Baron brought his hand cannon up and launched a compressed ball of Ki. The attack burst through the remaining few vines and he charged out through the new gap, his cannon already changing back into its sword form.

Rose ran through immediately after Baron, green light glowing over her staff as she prepared her spell.

Once they burst through into the daylight, Baron caught sight of his wife fading back into the shadow of one man. The man had collapsed, blood pouring out of his sides. There were three other men out front. They all seemed to wear some kind of miss matched pieces of armor, comprising a Kevlar vest, and pieces of Chiton covering their shoulders, legs and arms.

The three men—who weren't bleeding out—all held M4-carbines. They were firing where Kassandra had been. Baron used their distraction to his advantage as he charged in. Before he could reach them, a mass of roots erupted from the ground and entangled the men, causing them to stumble and trip.

The reptiles took that opportunity, at the mental prodding of Rose, to charge in. Apophis latched on to the gun arm of one man and immediately coiled itself around him. The beardies couldn't do much in the way of damage, but they aided the root spell by grabbing onto the ankles of the other two men and chewed on them. Their tiny teeth couldn't penetrate the armor, but it provided an extra bit of distraction.

Rose made sure Balder stayed in to protect the children. She didn't want the kids out where bullets were flying.

85

The fire mage managed to down a potion that stopped his bleeding before he raised a wand in his hand and pointed it at Baron. A bolt of condensed fire flew at Baron, but he simply cut it in half with his Ki-infused blade.

The fire mage's eyes grew wide in panic Baron followed through with his block, reversing the swing and going right for the caster's head. One gunman managed to tear through the roots holding him in place, and he shoulder checked Baron just before the swing could connect. It threw Baron off balance and he stumbled past. Baron grunted in pain as a three-round burst struck him in the back. Each round managed to penetrate his Ki enhanced natural armor, causing blood to spray out from his back and knock him all the way to the ground.

Kassandra re-appeared in the shadow of the man who'd shot her husband, stabbing him right in the kidney before vanishing a second later.

A loud crash, immediately followed by a pained yelp from Balder, caused Rose to spin around. An enormous figure, at least seven-feet-tall, came stomping out of the convenience store, holding Drake and Kassie dangling by their necks. The figure was wearing what looked like a suit of Fallout knockoff power armor. It was big, bulky, and felt powerful.

The poor kids were holding onto his forearms, trying to keep their weight off of their necks. A man's voice sounded out, slightly distorted as though it came from a loudspeaker. "Stop! Put down your weapons and kneel on the ground. If you don't, I'll snap one of the kid's necks like a twig."

Rose instantly dropped her staff and fell to her knees. She knew she couldn't do much, anyway. She only had a few spells, and the only one that had any direct combat application was her root spell. She could talk to animals mentally, see in the dark, and use a minor regeneration spell, but that was about it.

The rest of the men broke free of the entangling roots. One of them pulled out a set of handcuffs and forced Baron's hand behind his back while another kneeled on his neck. As soon as the cuffs were on him, the sword form reverted to looking like a gauntlet and went limp. They dragged him over next to Rose and forced him to his knees.

"Where is the other one?" the guy in the power armor asked.

"Captain, we don't know. She has shadow powers and keeps vanishing," one man answered.

"You have to the count of three to appear and kneel on the ground or the little girl dies. One. Two—" he paused in his counting as a mass of sparks fly off of his back. Kassandra had appeared behind him, trying to stab him in what looked like a gap in his armor. Before she could vanish again or do anything else, he swung around with Drake still in his hand and hit Kassandra with her own son.

Drake cried out in pain, and he knocked Kassandra to the side. The man placed his heavy, power-armored boot on her back, making her writhe in pain.

"Damn fucking lizard," a man behind Rose cried. A series of gunshots followed it. Rose jerked her head around and saw, to her horror, that her bearded dragons had both been killed, along with her husband's snake. Tears welled up in her eyes as she slumped.

"You will let the kids go, or so help me—" Baron was saying, before they had clubbed him behind the head with the stock of a carbine.

"Kill him," the captain said. The man who clubbed Baron carried his order out. He brought up his gun. It started glowing blue before it unleashed a torrent of rounds. Each bullet found its mark, splattering Baron's gray matter, blood, and bone all over the ground.

Rose gasped and tried to cry out before she was backhanded across the face. "Shut up, bitch."

Rose cradled her face. She feared he might have broken something. The strike had taken off almost fifteen Health. Out of the corner of her eye, she saw Balder. He was dragging one of his hind legs, but still trying to make his way to the children. A dedicated protector to the end.

"You will each put one of these collars around your neck. For each of you who refuses, a child will die," The captain declared. Drake and Kassie were both crying. The captain had yet to put them down.

One soldier dropped a black metallic collar on the cement in front of Rose. Looking back at the kids dangling in the captain's grip. She quickly used Identify on the collar.

Suppression Collars, Minor
These Collars are capable of suppressing any energy-based abilities regardless of the Path of Power chosen. Any energy regeneration is halted. Stamina recovery is

It's over. We're captured, and our freedom's at an end. Rose thought as she brought the device up to her own neck. She noticed Balder still trying to creep over. They might have been captured, but that didn't mean Balder had to be. All her other pets were dead. Balder could survive.

At the moment before she clicked the collar in place, she sent out a mental command to her Soul-Bound Familiar. *'Run. Run away from here, boy. Protect yourself. Stay safe.'*

She felt Balder's resistance to the idea. He didn't want to leave her or the kids. Rose had to think fast to come up with a way that would get him to listen. He was a good boy, but like all huskies, he was stubborn.

Go find John. Find John boy. John can help us. Rose included a mental image of her husband to reinforce the command. She pushed hard, and Balder finally obeyed. He limped away, ears laid back against his head and tail tucked between his legs. Rose let out a sigh as no one paid any attention to the dog. She let the collar click in place and lost all access to her Mana.

Thank you for reading Initialization: Family Perils, an Initialization side story. I hope you enjoyed it. There are plenty more to come. Please don't forget to rate and review. If you would like updates, you can join me on my Facebook page.

https://www.facebook.com/pathsofpower.initialization

or my website

www.authorseanbarber.com

You can also catch up on chapters on my Royalroad page:

https://www.royalroad.com/fiction/42922/paths-of-power-initialization

Or my Patreon, if you wish to support me further. All Patreon proceeds go towards future book publications. This includes Cover art, Editing, and any other Paths of Power related expenses that can improve your experience.

https://www.patreon.com/pathsofpowerseries

LitRPGs is a rapidly growing genre. If you would like to know more and interact with other fans and authors, you can check out these Facebook groups.

LitRPG Society: https://www.facebook.com/groups/LitRPGsociety/

LitRPG Books: https://www.facebook.com/groups/LitRPG.books/

LitRPG Group: https://www.facebook.com/groups/LitRPGGroup/

LitRPG and Gamelit Readers: https://www.facebook.com/groups/940262549853662/

For those Cultivation fans: https://www.facebook.com/groups/WesternWuxia/

The Gamelit Society: https://www.facebook.com/groups/GameLitSociety/

LitRPG Forum: https://www.facebook.com/groups/litrpgforum/

LitRPG Legion: https://www.facebook.com/groups/litrpglegion